# Playing with Fire

## Michele Sims

Playing with Fire. Copyright © 2019 by Michele Sims.



ISBN 978-1-7347567-1-5 print book
ISBN 978-1-7347567-0-8 ebook



Publisher: Green Books Publishers

Editing:  Nick May

Cover Design:  J. L. Woodson
jlwoodson@woodsonstudio.com

# TABLE OF CONTENTS

# CHAPTER ONE

A narrow ray of light escaped from the elevator as I looked through the small opening at Lecia, wide-eyed with panic, pressing as many buttons as she could on the elevator's panel to find the open-door button to release my foot, which was trapped between the doors. The alarm began blaring and she briefly covered her ears before resuming her frantic attempt to get the doors to open. The car jolted upward a few inches before coming to a complete stop, but the doors still didn't open.

"Cade don't worry. I'll free you," she yelled above the alarm and continued pressing buttons. Finally the doors opened, and the alarm went silent. I walked into the elevator, knowing my presence wasn't completely welcomed, but at least I was assured she still cared about my safety.

"Thanks. It was beginning to hurt." I wiggled my foot inside my favorite fine Italian leather shoe, which now had deep indentation marks on both sides. "I forgot before I stuck my foot in the door that this is a historic building without modern safety features, such as an automatic elevator door release."

Lecia turned her gaze upward and looked at the lighted red numbers as the doors closed completely and the car ascended to the floor of our rented apartment. She was still angry and feigned a lack of interest in anything I had to say.

"At least look at me, even if you don't have anything to say. We need to talk about what happened at the concert tonight."

"You're right on one account Cade, I have nothing to say to you."

"So it's my fault that another man was hitting on you, my wife, while I was on the stage earning a living for my family—our family?" She looked down and tightened her lips to prevent words from escaping, but it was obvious from the twitch of her lips she couldn't hold back the tide of her irritation any longer.

"Your hostility and demand that he be escorted out of the club were so over the top Cade. He was commenting on my dress and how nice I looked in it, something you have yet to do after I bought it specifically for your birthday celebration tonight. The man told me he was a fashion designer and beautiful clothing was his passion!"

"And you believed that? You're telling me that you felt there was no inclination on his part to admire the woman in the dress? Was he buying drinks for the dress or for you?" I leaned over and hit the emergency stop button, halting the car and setting off the alarm again.

"I don't believe you Cade."

The elevator phone buzzed, and I picked up the receiver.

"Bonjour, Jean-Claude. Yes, I hit the wrong button. So, if I hit the button to the left of it, the car will start moving again? Merci. Au revoir." I pursed my lips at her and placed the receiver back in the cradle.

"Cade, just start the car—or are you planning on holding me hostage?"

"Will you talk to me when we get in the apartment?"

"I told you I have nothing more to say to you." She tried starting the elevator, but it still didn't move. "Why aren't we moving?"

"You have to put in the code or start it with a key before pressing the release button."

"What's the code?" She swung her head and frowned at me.

"I'd tell you if you were talking to me, but you're not interested in anything I have to say." I began looking at the red numbers just as she had done minutes before.

"You can be so infuriating sometimes, but if you want to discuss the matter, then fine, we can, and I don't plan to filter what I have to say."

"I've never asked you to lie or mislead me Lecia, and you know it. I didn't know you were coming to the concert tonight, and you know I never celebrate my birthday when I'm on the road. I prefer to focus on business, get paid, and come home to my family."

"That's the narrative you like to believe, but you looked like you were having fun tonight, with dancers rubbing their asses against the birthday boy and the backup singers sounding like they were out of breath with desire as they sang to you to celebrate your special day. I don't think there was any mistaking that you were enjoying the show, judging by the bright smile on your face—until you looked out at the VIP section and saw me sitting there. I wouldn't have come if the other wives hadn't begged me to. They thought it would be fun. The man you insulted was buying all the women at the table drinks, not just me. He placed his arms around me to help me recover my shawl."

"All so perfectly innocent, was it? Why is his card in your bag? I saw him place it in there just before I interrupted your little party."

"What are you talking about?" She opened her purse and the card was on top.

"No one takes what's mine, and he disrespected me by continuing to hit on you after you told him your name— Lecia Moore—who coincidently was sitting at a table reserved for Cade Moore. You don't think he figured out you were my wife?"

"He didn't have to figure it out. I told him you were my husband and he said that didn't mean I couldn't have friends. Oh!" She tightened her shoulders and fisted her hands to her side. "Let's not do this here. I concede your point, but it's no excuse for your rudeness. We need to get to the apartment and relieve Angelique. She's babysitting Miles tonight since Madame Marcel was sick."

"Fine." I punched in the code, pressed the release button, and started the elevator moving again. The door opened on our floor and I quickly placed my hand on the small of her back to escort her to our apartment.

"I'm sorry if I embarrassed you but not sorry if I offended him. I've seen him before and he's one of those men who thinks his money and looks excuse his bad behavior."

"So you're saying you personally know of men who use their looks and money to treat women like they are objects?"

"Don't be funny. I'm sorry I upset you, but you know how jealous I get, especially when you're the most smoking-hot woman in the room. The audience likes the surprise birthday boy gimmick. It's all a marketing ploy. Sometimes we recognize audience members celebrating birthdays to make the shows more intimate and to engage the audience. The women in my employ are professionals, and unlike the wives who make sure they come to every show, you know I would never be unfaithful to you. I have eyes for only one woman, and I was lucky enough to capture her attention and her heart." We stopped outside the door and she allowed me to turn her head and plant a kiss on her lips.

"Do you have your keys Cade? Mine seem to be buried in my bag."

"Yes, I have them right here." I dug into my pocket and placed the keys into the lock. Lecia pushed open the door and followed the sounds of Angelique's voice into the room off the foyer.

I followed behind her and we both stopped to observe Miles, now seven years old, nestled in the oversized chair against Angelique's voluptuous breast with eyes fixed on her face instead of on the book she was reading to him.

"Bonsoir, Monsieur and Madame Moore. We were just finishing our book. Did you enjoy your evening?"

"Yes, we did, Angelique. Forgive me for asking, but that dress wasn't what you were wearing earlier was it?" Lecia furrowed her brow while looking at the two of them.

"No Madame. I just changed my dress. I have a late date with my boyfriend tonight." She untangled herself from Miles and got up out of the chair to pull down the hem of her dress before she came forward for her pay.

"I've got it Lecia." I reached into my wallet and pulled out the biggest bill I had to pay young Angelique for her services. *Wow, Lecia really trusts me. I know some women would never employ a beautiful twenty-something woman to come into their home.*

"Does this cover it?" I handed her the money.

"Merci, Monsieur. You're very generous."

"Yes, my Cade is a very generous man. Thank you, Angelique, and don't let us hold you up."

"Call me any time Madame."

"Mami, Angelique can read faster than Madame Marcel and she doesn't need to find her glasses." Angelique giggled as she went back to the chair and bent over Miles to kiss him on both cheeks.

"You're such a sweet boy." I looked at Lecia scowling as she looked briefly at me viewing Angelique's rear end with a furtive glance and at Miles smiling as he got a view of Angelique's ample mounds showing above the top of her dress.

"Au revoir, all." Angelique turned to leave the apartment.

"Au revoir, Angelique. See you later." Miles waved as she exited the room and headed for the front door.

"Miles, you should have been dressed for bed by now." Lecia took her shawl from around her shoulders and placed it on the chair.

"Did you and Angelique sort out the toys you will be taking with you?"

"Where are the two of you going, Lecia?" Her remark had piqued my interest. I headed to the bar for a glass of seltzer.

"Mami, we were too busy reading and playing soldiers to pack. I'll do it later when Angelique comes back tomorrow."

I unscrewed the cap on the bottle and poured a little seltzer in a glass.

"Where are the two of you going? On an overnight tour of the countryside? I think it would be good to see a little more of France than just stay in the city." I looked at Lecia.

"Mami, you were happy tonight after you called Angelique. You'll be happy again if you call Angelique tomorrow, or if you like, I can place the person making you so sad on my list. I told you I'll take care of it." Lecia briefly closed her eyes and held her head in her palms before joining me at the bar for a large glass of wine.

"You don't usually drink this late Lecia. What's going on? Where are you going?"

"I'm not used to having a three-way conversation this time of night. Miles, I won't be going anywhere tomorrow.

I need to organize our things to ship them back to the States. I told you to gather the toys you wanted to take on the plane with you. Now go and get ready for bed."

My mouth dropped open as the news of Lecia's plans to leave me in Paris unfolded. She took a sip of wine and still hadn't answered any of my questions.

"But Mami, I told you I'd take care of everything and I want to see Angelique again." He stomped his feet and crossed his arms in front of his chest. *What in the hell is going on here?*

"Miles Moore, go and go now." She pointed towards the door and took another sip of wine.

"Mami, I hate you," he yelled, turning red. He stared at Lecia while she looked at the both of us nonplussed and took another sip of her wine. She said nothing, and Miles broke the standoff by stomping toward the door.

"Miles, stop." I'd had enough of his insolent behavior.

"Cade let him go. It's late and he doesn't do well when he's cranky and tired." I shook my head and chose to ignore her request.

"No I need to handle this now. Turn around Miles and face me now. I don't like your behavior one bit. I get it you're angry, but your language is unacceptable, young man. Unacceptable and I won't tolerate it. Calm down and tell me what's going on." *Somebody sure as hell needs to tell me what's going on.* I took a seat in the closest chair and Lecia took a chair while she continued to sip from her glass.

"Mami has been crying for a couple of days," he pondered, placing his index finger to the side of his lips. "I think for a couple of days, but I know she has been crying more than just yesterday. Somebody made her sad and some women came over and told her to go out with them. I told her I would place the bad person on my list and take care of them, but she told me no. She called Madame Marcel and Angelique came over instead because Madame Marcel was sick. I really like Angelique."

"Yes Miles, but you haven't told me why you would talk to your mother the way you did."

"Mami was sad before I told her I hated her yesterday."

"Miles, you're telling me you've said this before? Lecia, you didn't tell me about Miles's bad behavior." My chest heaved as I spoke and looked at them both.

"But Dad, you told me you should be true to your feelings. I was expressing my feelings like Hermie did when he was mad with his mother."

"Who is Hermie?" I looked at both of them while Lecia placed her glass on the table and finally spoke.

"Hermie is a cartoon character on a popular show here. He's copying Hermie and has said it ever since we watched the episode two days ago. Miles, go to bed. We're all too tired for this right now."

"You won't be watching Hermie anymore until you understand what is appropriate for this household, Mijo."

"Yes Daddy." He turned and walked out the door in seconds to make sure I wouldn't get up to physically escort him to his room. I calmed down before I addressed my questions to Lecia. I wasn't in the mood to search too hard or too long for answers.

"Are you planning on taking Miles and leaving me?"

"Cade, I'm tired and I don't want to argue with you."

"I'm tired too, but I think I deserve some answers." All of this was landing on me like a ton of emotional bricks. My chest was tight; and I could hardly breathe, but I had to know.

"Are you leaving me? Have you been angry with me before the incident tonight?"

"I'm not leaving you. I'm leaving the tour because this isn't working for me any longer. I've been supportive of your desire to tour and spread your music. I don't want to stop you from doing something you obviously love, but I can't do this anymore." She placed her hand over her mouth and turned away from me but not before I saw her tears falling.

"Lecia, give me six more months. I can't change my tour schedule before then. You realize this affects more than the three of us. My band and their families are depending on me."

"I understand that Cade, and that's why I felt we could weather a separation for four to six months. The separation may also help to put things in perspective for both of us."

"Why were you crying if you thought your decision was a good one?"

"I was feeling a little overwhelmed—and because I've been trying to deal with Miles, who you know can be a handful sometimes. I'm onboard with our decision to allow him to express his feelings, and I'll admit it stung a lot when he said he hated me the first time, but I realized he was only copying the character on tv. I've tried to talk to you about all of this, but you're either busy composing music, practicing for your next performance, or sleeping. You haven't been there for us for months now. I didn't see any reason to stay other than to share your bed."

"Stay to share my life Lecia. We share our lives with each other."

"Well, your life has gotten pretty crowded. You don't even know what's going on with your son under your own roof."

"No, I admit I don't know about his list and I haven't witnessed his disobedience before." I took in a breath and dropped my head in shame. I wouldn't deny that I had allowed my career to overshadow my responsibilities as a husband and father.

"We've had several caretakers to allow me a few hours a week to leave the apartment by myself for my own sanity, and every time I leave, there's something else I have to deal with waiting for me. I've had the security team search the apartment several times and no matches or lighters have been found yet, but when I return, there's always a smoky or sulfur smell, as if something has been burning. I've had to fire many nannies and take Miles out of school because unexplained fires occurred at his school. They didn't blame him, but I got the sense they were secretly delighted when I called to tell them he wouldn't be returning. Madame Marcel assures me he spends most of his free time playing with his soldiers or watching tv, but there have been times I returned and smelled her strong rose perfume probably covering the scent of fire. She loves Miles and I know she would do anything to keep her job." I pulled my chair close to her and took her hands in mine.

"We need to solve this problem together. I can't help if I'm thousands of miles away."

"Dana, your parents, and my parents will help me. Dana and the kids are coming to London to join Vincent while he's in Europe working on a project. They were going to visit the sights in London before coming here to Paris for a few days. I plan to join her on the trip home and having the kids around will make it easier for Miles to say goodbye to you. I'm aware this won't be easy for any of us."

"So you decided on all of this without talking to me about it?" I maintained my voice as low and even as I could. Exploding in anger wasn't going to help the situation.

"When Cade? You tell me when I should have discussed this with you. You've been gone for days and only returned earlier tonight to change before going to your show. You kissed us goodbye and poof, you were gone again."

"I'll own my part in this Lecia, but I don't think your decision to leave is the only decision that can be made. Alright, I'll not pressure you about this, but what about this list Miles is talking about?"

"He keeps talking about powers he has to make my enemies go away. He thinks someone is hurting me and that's why I'm crying. He asked me for names and I had to turn my face away to stop from laughing when he asked how to spell the names. You haven't noticed he walks around at times with a notebook?"

"I gave him the notebook to write down new words he discovered and wanted to remember."

"Well, he also has a page for names to settle scores. When I didn't tell him a name, that's when he told me he hated me for the first time. He told me he couldn't help me if I didn't give him the names."

"Lecia, this is disturbing, and I don't like it one bit."

"I agree, and I want to surround him with people who love him to ward off these angry feelings he's developing. I may need to get him some professional help." She looked up and I turned to see Miles entering the room in his pajamas.

"I brushed my teeth and I need my hug before I go to bed, Mami. Hold me tight so I can feel your love and I'll hug you to give you mine." He ran to his mother and embraced her tightly as she placed kisses on his cheek.

"I love you and adore you Mami."

"I love and adore you too Miles." He turned and was about to leave the room.

"No love for Dad, Mijo? Is the word adore, one of your new words? I haven't heard you use it before." He came into my outstretched arms and I took him into a tight embrace.

"That felt so good Mijo. I felt the love."

"Dad, I could feel your love too. Yes, adore is one of my new words. I liked the sound of it and it seemed right for Mami."

"Miles, I love you and I know you're better than some cartoon character named Hermie. I don't want you to act like him anymore. His words hurt people." He listened and tilted his head before he spoke.

"I wouldn't hurt Mami. I love her, and I'll always protect her."

"Don't worry about protecting her. That's my job Miles."

"Alright, you can handle it when you're here." He yawned, and I tightened my lips, having been indicted and found guilty by both family members.

"Goodnight Miles." I hugged him again and he returned my embrace.

"Go get under the covers and I'll be there shortly to tuck you in and kiss you goodnight, one last time."

"Okay Mami." He ran off, leaving Lecia with a way out of this current discussion, which had stalled at an impasse.

"We all need to get some rest. I'll join you in the bedroom after I say goodnight to Miles."

"I agree we need to sleep on it and talk about it in the morning."

"Stop looking at me like that, Cade." I was lying on the bed letting my eyes travel down her body as she unzipped her dress and placed it on the chair. I licked my lips slowly for emphasis.

"You know exactly what I'm talking about. You're looking at me like you're planning on ravaging my body. We both agreed it was late and we needed to get some rest."

"I'm enjoying looking at my wife. Is that a crime?" I continued to let my eyes travel the length of her body. "Are you wearing a new bra and panty set for my birthday?"

She placed her hands on her hips and flung her head, letting her hair fall to the side.

"You didn't notice I was wearing a new dress but now you're commenting on my underwear that looks like other sets I own?"

"First of all, I may not comment on your outfits all the time because I feel your outerwear is for other people and your underwear, which is new and different, is for me. Your bra is a darker red than the one you have like it and cut a little lower, with less lace, and your hi-cut panties have little hearts on them. How is that for being observant?" She looked down at her underwear to confirm my observations.

"You're right about it I guess, but time is up birthday boy. I'm tired."

"Come here Lecia." I flexed my index finger, bidding her to come to me. "I want a closer look at you before I go shower, and please, take your time getting here. You know I love the sexy way you walk when you've gotten some wine in you." She swayed her hips and at a slow pace, walked to me.

"That's it baby. Just like that." I placed a pillow over my groin to cover the evidence of my excitement. She stopped midway and placed her hands on her hips, which she rolled slowly in front of me.

"That was some good wine. Thanks for getting it for me."

"The brand came highly recommended and I bought it for you a week ago. Nothing but the best for my baby. Let's not let good wine go waste. Come here girl."

She crawled into bed and plopped beside me, wearing a sweet smile on her face. I removed the pillow before sliding close to her and took her into my arms.

"The silk of your underwear feels so soft." I rubbed my hands along her breast and down to her panties.

"Yes it does feel good, and I know what you're doing."

"I'm admiring your vision of loveliness. What are you accusing me of now?"

"You're hoping the wine will kick in and I'll turn into a freak." She giggled and placed her arms around my neck. I took it as an invitation to place kisses down her neck and pushed the material covering her breast to the side to pull on the nipple of her breast just the way she liked it. Her eyes were beginning to dilate as I grabbed her ass and increased the friction between us as I rotated my hips against hers.

"This is how we're meant to be each and every night. Your body seeking and giving pleasure to mine. I don't do well without your physical presence." I plunged my tongue into her mouth to prevent her from responding and pulled on her lips to draw her breath into mine as if I were a man fighting to claim my position as her lover. I wanted her to want me as much as I wanted her. There could be no question that she would be in my bed every night where she belonged. She panted as I released her from the kiss.

"You're not fighting fair, Cade," she took in a deep breath and exhaled.

"I'm not fighting you. I'm showing how much I love you and need you. Hug me tight so I can feel how much you love me." She took me into her arms and I placed my head against her breast while she stroked my head. I took her hand and placed it against my heart, beating wildly in my chest.

"This is what you do to me. It scares the shit out of me to think you want to separate from me for even a couple of months. Besides, it's my birthday and you won't let me enjoy you while I have the chance."

"Stop the bullshit Cade." She untangled herself from me and got up to take off her bra and get under the covers. I followed suit and took off my briefs.

"Good night baby." She reached up and turned off her lamp as I sat up in bed, fuming with irritation and lust.

"Cade, aren't you going to turn off your lights?"

I reached over and dimmed the lights, refusing to join her under the covers. She looked up at me, and after observing the sadness in my eyes, threw off the covers and came to sit in my lap face to face.

"It's obvious you need to say something to me. So let's get it out in the open." She insisted, and I placed my hands alongside her hips to steady her as she sat over me in a cowgirl position.

"I need to be inside you to gather my thoughts. There are a lot of things swirling through my head right now."

"Is that so?" She lifted her hips as I pulled her panties to the side and placed my hardened penis slowly inside her. "Is that better?" She gazed in my eyes and settled on top of me.

"Yes, it's an improvement." I began rolling my hips. Her breasts grabbed my attention as they swayed to the rhythm of my gyration. I finally muttered something as I struggled to connect my words in a coherent sentence.

"I don't want to worry about us." I looked up at her as she threw her head back and placed her hands on my shoulders while she moved up and down on my cock, moistened with her juices. I smiled, watching her trying to respond to me.

"There…is nothing…to worry…about. Oh, Cade. What are…what are…you doing to me?"

I continued to thrust and hoped I could get her to change her mind.

"Why would you deny me…oh shit…the pleasure of your body?" I was crazed with lust, and I growled before I took her nipple, one then the other, into my mouth and pulled hard. I knew she loved the slight pain heightening her pleasure. Her back was arched, and I placed my fingers between her legs to play with her clit.

"Stop it," she screamed, and I pulled back. "Don't stop," and I resumed my play with more fervor while we bounced up and down on the bed. I turned our bodies to the side abruptly but braced her as she landed on her back and took her over the edge with her legs wrapped tightly around my waist. I rolled off her and held her hand in the quiet of our room while staring up at the ceiling. Lecia was the first to break the silence.

"We'll be alright Cade, if I'm here or if I'm thousands of miles away in the States. I now know what else you need me to say."

"What is it oh wise one?" I smiled and turned my head to look at her.

"You need me to say I love you and you're the only one who can ignite my body with passion the way you just did."

"I know that Lecia. I don't doubt our physical bond." I laughed, and she snuggled closer and settled in my arms.

"Most importantly, you need to hear if you need me, I'll be on the first plane to return to you. I'll need time to get Miles settled, but your place in my life is of importance to me, and neither time nor distance will diminish that. My heart beats for you, and I'm crushing on you more than the first time I told you I loved you. You must admit I only agreed to a one year, max two years of touring with you, and here we are, six years later. Most of our time together has been on a series of tours. Cade, I just can't do it any longer." I held her tighter.

"I know, but I can't say I feel great knowing you and my boy will be leaving soon."

"I'll give you a grade A for trying to change my decision with the mind fuck."

"I'll take the A for my skills, but I've never fucked you before. I only know how to make love to my queen. We haven't been apart for more than a few days since we started living together years ago."

"We're strong Cade. We'll get through this together. I have no doubts about it."

We got under the covers and I continued stroking her back until she fell asleep. I didn't like it, but I had to accept there wasn't much I could do to change her mind.

Michele Sims

# CHAPTER TWO

The band had a much-needed break in our concert schedule and I decided to spend it at home working on a new composition instead of going in to Club Le Rouge to practice with them. Lecia was sleeping in while I got up to feed Miles. We ate our usual ugly pancakes, my specialty, and went to the den. Miles normally played on the floor with his toy soldiers while I composed at my desk.

"Pow, pow…pow, pow, pow. I will destroy you with my fire rockets. Pow." I watched as he slammed his hand into several flanks of soldiers he had meticulously arranged. Normally, his play was less aggressive, and he preferred spending time setting up strategies used in famous battles. His favorite general for the moment was Hannibal Barca, the Carthaginian general. It took us a long time to locate toy elephants for him to use in setting up one of Hannibal's famous battles, and now he was blowing them up and tossing his toys around the room.

"Miles, Daddy is trying to concentrate. Can you play a little quieter?"

"But Daddy, battles are never quiet. You and Mami weren't quiet when you battled each other last night." I put down my pen, no longer interested in drawing musical notes on my sheet.

"Did you hear me and Mami talking last night?"

"You weren't talking. You were yelling, and she was telling you, stop Cade, don't stop Cade. Are you angry that we're going back to North Carolina? Why don't you come with us? You always say we're family and we should be together. Pow. Pow, pow." He turned his attention back to the battle between his soldiers.

"Come to Daddy, Miles. I want to talk to you." I extended my hands and hoisted him onto my lap.

"I'll be honest with you. I don't want you and Mami to leave me, but I understand why it's time for you two to go back to see Granddad, Grammy, Grammie Mommie, Abuela, Papi and Marissa. They're all getting older except your fun-loving Tia Marissa, and Mami wants to spend some time with them too. They miss you and they ache to see you again."

"They tell me that all the time on the phone. They tell me they love me, and they ache to see me. Why is love painful?"

"You're such a wise boy for someone so young, and that's a good question. Yes, love can be painful, especially when you're separated from the ones you love. My heart hurts when I'm separated from you and Mami because I love you so much. When you hug me, I feel so warm and my chest feels full. I guess my heart feels smaller when I'm not with you and aches to feel strong again."

"I know how that feels Daddy." I hugged him tightly.

"But guess what?" I looked into his eyes.

"What?" Miles placed his hand on my forearm.

"Even when Daddy has to work and be away from you, my heart beats so fast when I hear your voice and I feel so warm and good inside just by thinking about you. I wake up every morning excited and looking forward to the day we'll be together again. We can't be selfish with love Miles. We must spread it around. Granddad and Grammy loved me and told me how wonderful it would be when someday I had my own child. They prepared me to share love with you and we must give some of the love they gave to us back to them. You understand? They're part of our family too, and I want you to check on them until I come home, alright?"

"I understand Daddy, but if that's true, why were you angry with Mami last night?"

"I was upset because I didn't think I could live without you. I didn't want to feel what it was like coming to the apartment and you and Mami weren't here." I hugged him again and hid my face, hoping to tamp down the feelings rising in my throat and threatening to choke me.

"Don't worry. Mami told me that any time I wanted to see you, we would come back. I couldn't leave if she didn't promise me that. I'll be here when you need me just like you've been here for me."

"You and Mami are everything to me. We'll be together again. I promise."

"Mami said you have to honor your contacts. Your word is your bond."

"Yes, my contracts. I have to honor my contracts because for us Moore men, you and me, our word is our bond." I looked up and saw Lecia leaning against the door frame.

"Hi Mami. Daddy made pancakes for us and he said he wasn't mad at you anymore. You don't have to yell stop Cade anymore. He's not mad."

"What are you talking about Miles?" Lecia was turning deeper shades of red as she gathered the robe around her.

"He heard you talking to me last night. You were telling me to stop being mad."

"Yes. I was telling him not to be sad. We weren't fighting Miles. I'd better get dressed and then I need you to go to your room, so I can help you get dressed." She hurried out of the room, too embarrassed to explain our escapades last night to our son.

"If you'll be a little quieter, I can finish my work then we can spend a day of fun in Paris."

"Okay, and will Mami come with us?"

"I'm sure she will." He got back on the floor and started arranging his soldiers in battle formations. "I plan to take her to dinner tonight. Do you want to go out with us or do you want me to call Angelique?" He stopped playing for a moment, thought about it, and it didn't take him long decide.

"Have fun but make sure it's Angelique and not Madame Marcel."

"Deal." He got up and wrote on a piece of paper he took from my desk.

"Sign this contract Daddy, then I'll know you'll keep your word no matter what Mami says."

He slid the paper to me and on it in big letters I read, Miles Has a Date with Angel Tonight.

"Let me text her and make sure she's available." She responded immediately; and I turned the face of my phone to him, so he could see her response.

**Angelique**: Oui

I captured the biggest and most captivating smile spreading across Miles's face with the camera on my phone. He was only seven years old, but he surely looked like a young man who was smitten and crushing on an attractive young women.

The screen on my computer remained blank as I hadn't made any progress on my newest composition despite the use of state-of-the-art professional notation software. I couldn't blame Miles, who was between my legs looking at the cursor blinking at both of us. He was a needed distraction as I coped with my writer's block. I'd had a hit with the song Mijo but couldn't seem to come up with enough music to finish the album I hoped to release before the end of the year.

"What's this Daddy?" He hit one of the presets labeled "Lecia" and her voice on high volume filled the room.

"I love you Cade. I'll always love you Cade."

"Miles, this isn't a toy. Please don't play with Daddy's equipment, and I've told you before, you have to be quiet when Daddy's working."

"Alright Daddy, I'll be quiet, shush." He placed his index finger to his mouth and turned down the volume on the computer, allowing Lecia's voice to sound like a sweet whisper. I smiled and repeated the sound at the same volume—I was getting the inspiration I needed. I moved Miles to the side, so he could lean against my desk as notes flowed from my head to the computer screen. I completed a stanza of music and picked up my saxophone before connecting the sound of Lecia's voice to my playing. It was dope, and Miles was bobbing his head to the music as I played. I was on to something. I wrote a few more notes to record and attached the remaining part of Lecia's recorded voice to the end of the song: "I'll always love you."

"I like it Daddy. That's a good song."

"Thanks, I couldn't have written it without you."

"Without me and Mami. She always tells me to never forget that she loves me. Does she tell you that too?"

"Yeah she does. We're two lucky men to have Mami." I rubbed his head and he nodded in agreement.

"Go find her so she can help you get dressed while I finish my work."

"Okay but don't forget your promise. I want to play with Angelique tonight."

I gave him a thumbs up as he ran out of the room. It crossed my mind that I forgot to ask him about the list Lecia said he was keeping, but I needed to finish the composition while I was in a creative zone. *Love, love, love.* That was always the key that unlocked my creativity. I considered myself a lucky man to have love given freely to me to transmit to thousands through my music. I relaxed, letting the song "Whispers of Love" flow out of me and onto the page.

# CHAPTER THREE

"Dana, I'm so glad you and the kids are finally here. Come on in." There was no mistaking the pure joy in Lecia's voice as she opened the door with a bright smile spreading across her face and she began hugging Dana and the children. Miles and I were seated on the couch, busy looking at cartoons on tv, any cartoon except Hermie. He saw Aria running towards him and the popcorn in his lap flew out of the bowl and into the air as his attention turned to greeting his favorite cousin instead of enjoying a snack with me.

"Miles!" everyone exclaimed in unison. My brother's family was a loving, gregarious bunch who filled any room with bright smiles and gaiety.

"There's popcorn everywhere." Lexie giggled, along with her siblings. They were happy to reunite with their cousin and laugh at the sight of popcorn confetti landing around the room. I was a bit irritated I would have to clean up the mess. I got on my knees and swept as much of it into the bowl as quickly as possible while Miles ran to greet Aria, barreling at full speed to grab him. The two of them embraced first, followed by a heartfelt welcoming of his other cousins and his Aunt Dana, who also came to greet me.

"Hi Cade." Dana came and hugged me after standing in the line for hugs with her children.

"Hi Dana. Glad to see you all again." I was trying hard to mask the mixed feelings of seeing them again, which also meant my time with Lecia and Miles was growing short.

"We're here for you too Cade. Please remember that." Dana tried to reassure me.

I nodded and turned to comment on the growth of each child as at least a year had passed since I'd seen my brother's family. Dana and Lecia were busy catching up with each other while I engaged in conversation with the kids. Alex was a teenager and was connected to his headphones, which Vincent had told me had become electronic extensions of his ears.

"So Alex, I'm surprised you decided to come along to see your uncle."

"I missed you Unc. You know you're one of my favorite peeps. The old man told me to come check on you." We fist bumped each other.

"I'm glad you came. I missed you too, and you're really getting taller, but I probably could still beat you in a game of basketball."

"Nah, I don't think so. You probably couldn't beat Austin without puffing. My little brother is developing some mad skills on the court. He's playing with the junior varsity team at his school already." Austin was nine years old and had gotten taller too. He blushed as his older brother, his idol, complimented him.

"Austin, your Dad told me how good you've gotten with your sports. Are you still practicing your drums?" I introduced all the children to music, including the twins, when they were three years old.

"Yes, I still like the drums, and Mom enrolled me in a dance class to improve my artistry on the court." He rolled his eyes and his mother piped in.

"Well, it has helped, and your coach said so. He was so impressed that he recommended dance class to the other boys, some of whom have enrolled in your class."

"And how is my little ballerina, speaking of dance? You're still as pretty as ever Lexie." She was twelve years old and still able to wrap her father around her fingers.

"Thanks Uncle Cade. I really like my dance class, and I've been selected to dance in several performances this year. I hope you'll be home in time to see at least one of them."

"I'll try Lexie. Send me your schedule, ok?"

"I will." She and Austin settled back on the couch with me, and Lecia brought a fresh bowl of popcorn for us to enjoy while we watched tv.

A show lasting half an hour had begun and ended since Aria and Miles left to go to his room. I hadn't said much to Aria, Austin's twin sister since their arrival, and a nagging feeling that I needed to check on them wouldn't leave me alone.

"I'll be right back." I kissed Lexie, who was leaning against me, on the forehead and gave her the bowl of popcorn to share with her brothers. "Let me go check on Miles and Aria."

The door was ajar, and I couldn't help listening before going in. They were on the floor setting up his toy soldiers and didn't notice I was peering in on them.

"I really missed you Miles."

"I missed you too Aria, but I'm going to miss my daddy."

"The time will go by fast. I miss my daddy when he's gone too, but we'll keep busy having fun together." He nodded but the sad eyes and downturned lips belied that he didn't seem convinced of the benefit of time.

"I heard my Mommy talking to Tia Lecia, and she said you said something horrible. Did you say you hated your mother?"

"I said it, but I didn't mean it." Miles lowered his eyes.

"Well why did you say it? I hope you said you were sorry and would never say it again."

"I don't think I said I was sorry, but I haven't said it again. I was angry, that's all."

"Miles, some kids at school said mean things to me and I thought they were my friends. They hurt my feelings and I didn't want to go back to that school. My mother and Grammie have been teaching me at home."

"Don't worry about them Aria. When I get to North Carolina, I'll take care of them. You're family, and we look out for each other, just like Grammie Mommy always says."

"I don't worry about them anymore. Grammie Mommy always said we should be kind to each other. I'll always love you, but you can't be my best friend if you're not kind."

"You're my best friend and I'll say sorry for you." He started to get up off the floor and I backed away from the door.

"Nope, you shouldn't do it for me. You have to do it for you." My wise little Aria made some points with Miles. Vincent and Dana were doing a good job with their kids, I had to admit, as I returned to the front room of the apartment. Austin and Lexie were still on the couch while Alex was in the corner jamming to the music plugged into his ears. Miles and Aria came into the room and Miles stopped and faced his mother.

"I'm sorry I said I hated you Mami. I didn't mean it and I hope you forgive me."

Lexie and Austin's jaws dropped as they looked at Miles. Alex, the elder statesman, had unplugged his music in time to hear the public apology.

"That's not cool little dude. Your mom is good to you," he told him, and Miles dropped his head.

"I know Alex. I was wrong." Miles looked at his hands and avoided eye contact with Alex.

"Come here Miles." Lecia opened her arms to him and he went to her without hesitation.

"I accept your apology, and don't forget we have an agreement. I'll never forget you love me as long as you remember I'll always love you no matter what."

"I won't forget Mami, and I'm sorry not because Aria told me to apologize but because I was wrong and not being kind." He looked back at his cousin to make sure she understood his intentions.

"I know that Miles. Alex always tells me you and I are a lot alike. We're both stubborn and we don't feel we should do things just to please other people." Aria reassured him and gave him a hug around the shoulders.

"Lecia, we should be going. Our suite at the hotel across the street should be ready. Have you finished your packing? And will you all be able to join us in a brief trip around Paris?"

"Yes and we have tickets for a day trip to Austria. Cade has some time off and will be able to come along with us."

"Great. Kids let's get going. Lecia, I'll call you, so we can set a time to meet tomorrow. We loved spending time with Vincent in London, and I'm personally looking forward to seeing the sights in France. I know you don't want to go to the tourist traps again, and I'll understand if you and Cade want at least a day to yourselves before we leave."

"Things will work out, won't they Cade?" Lecia looked at me and I saw that she was concerned. *I thought my adjustment to her decision to leave Paris would have been easier by now. I guess there is nothing easy about saying goodbye to people you love.*

"Sure. I want to get in some time with my nieces and nephews while you're here. Call us later and we can get together for dinner," I piped in with a lighthearted tone to my voice.

"We'd love that." The kids were heading to the door and Miles was walking between Austin and Aria.

"Where are you going buddy?" He had his jacket in his hand.

"I'm going with them. I want to play with their toys."

"Miles, you have a room full of toys," I told him.

"It's alright with me Cade if it's alright with the two of you. Aria was so excited about seeing Miles, she barely slept last night."

"Same with Miles. They probably could both use a nap." Lecia chuckled.

"I'll call you after we get settled in. Bye you two." Dana corralled her brood and headed for the door.

"Miles, you be good and listen to your Aunt Dana."

"I will Daddy. See you later." He hugged me and his mother before running to the elevator with his cousins.

"Bye." I closed the door and gave Lecia a long, knowing look as I realized Lecia was right. Miles needed to spend time with his extended family and be around other kids. I tried, but I couldn't mask the look on my face as I stood immobilized by my own personal epiphany. I sighed as I had finally resolved some of my own inner conflicts about my family leaving Paris.

"I don't want us to be apart either, but I think you're finally seeing that it's time for Miles and me to go home." Lecia seemed to be reading my thoughts.

"It doesn't make it less sad for me that it's true and you're right." Lecia hugged me as I leaned on her for support.

"When is Miles coming back?" I picked at my lunch. Lecia had prepared one of my favorites, but I couldn't enjoy it as the hours ticked by on their final day in Paris.

"He should be back soon. He's just a block away with Angelique at their favorite bistro. She came and got him, so they could have a special goodbye and we could have some time alone together. Cade, this isn't easy for me either."

"I never thought it would be easy, but I just didn't realize it would be so hard." I looked down at my plate and moved my food around. I placed my fork on the table and got up.

"Do you mind going to the couch with me? I need to have you in my arms."

"You don't need to ask me for affection. We both need it right now." Lecia got up and joined me on the couch and placed her head on my chest. The warmth of her body and the steady beat of her heart was soothing to my heart, which was breaking under the prospect that in a few hours I would be alone in our little cocoon. Lecia had made it a home for me and Miles and she was leaving.

"I loved your new song. Thanks for playing it for me last night. It's probably going to be a hit. I can feel it. Miles was right that the song gives you happy feet. Did you see how much he danced and enjoyed the song while you were playing?" I smiled as I thought of him jumping around the room smiling and dancing.

"Cade, I don't say it enough, but you know how proud I am of you. It took me a while to not feel in competition with your music, but now, I know I'm in a good space to explore options for my life while you continue with the tour.

Miles is older, and with the help of family, maybe I can go back to work part time. I think having something of my own might be good for all of us. I don't want to grow into being a *Momster* and smother Miles."

"Lecia, I thought you were interested in adding to the family, and we could talk about having another child. We could work on it after I get off tour. Wouldn't that be good for all of us?" I smiled and raised my eyebrows.

"We can talk about it Cade, but I'm not interested in having another child while you're off somewhere on another continent."

"I'm considering doing some artist-in-residence tours where I would perform at the same venue for at least a year. There are opportunities out there other than Vegas for artists who want a break from touring." The doorbell rang, and I got up to answer it.

"That's probably Miles and Angelique."

Lecia followed me to the door and it was Angelique bringing Miles home; Miles who walked in with that same blissful look I'd captured a few days ago.

"Bonjour Monsieur Cade and Madame Lecia."

"Bonjour Angelique. How much do we owe you?"

"Nothing. You can't place a price on affection. I do this from my heart."

"Merci, Angelique. Miles has great affection for you too, and we're thankful for the time you've spent with him." Lecia acknowledged our gratitude and Angelique turned a brighter shade of pink.

"Ca me fait plaisir—you're welcome. I can't stay long because I have a class today and I need to get going. Miles, I'll miss him very much." She bent down to kiss him on both cheeks.

"Au revoir." Her eyes misted with tears.

"Au revoir, Angelique. I'll miss you too."

"Au revoir Angelique," Lecia and I joined in. We walked her to the door and I didn't close it until after she got inside the elevator car, still waving at us.

"Miles let's go get your personal things out of the bedroom. I want to make sure we separate it from the things the movers are going to deliver to our home in North Carolina."

"Alright Mami." They were on their way to his room when the doorbell rang again.

"I'll get it." I opened the door and Vincent was standing beside Dana and the kids.

"What are you doing here?" A smile spread across my face as I was swept up in a brotherly bear hug. "Come on in." His family came into the apartment while we remained talking at the door near the closet.

"Did I surprise you?"

"Yes, this is a surprise. Hey you guys." I extended greetings to everyone.

"Well, I'm here, Cade, because Aria left her favorite boots in London. I got to take in a ballet with Lexie at a matinee yesterday and a soccer game with everyone last night. How have you been?"

"I'll do. Today hasn't been the best day but it's not the worst either."

"It's not easy separating from your family." Vincent placed his hand on my shoulder.

"No it's not, but a man has to do whatever he needs to do to support his family," he reminded me.

"You're right." I called out to Miles and Lecia, who were still in his room. "Lecia, Miles; Dana and the kids are here—and a surprise."

"What's the surprise?" Miles came running out of his room to join us in the living area.

"Uncle Vincent!" He yelled and ran into his arms. "I know you brought me something. What is it?"

"Miles, your uncle doesn't have to give you something every time he sees you." Lecia gave Vincent a kiss on the cheek.

"I know he doesn't, but he always does." Miles remarked, and Vincent placed him on his feet before pulling out a soccer jersey rolled up in his jacket pocket.

"This is a signed jersey from one of my favorite soccer teams in England. Lexie and Aria didn't want one, but I got one for you, Alex, and Austin since you all play soccer."

"This is great! Thank you, Uncle Vincent." He held up the jersey and looked at the autograph.

"Are you ready to go Lecia?" Dana asked. "We need to leave a little early since traffic is heavy this time of day. Vincent talked to the bellman and he was going to send someone up to get your bags."

"Yes, we're ready. Miles, go get your backpack."

"Are you going back to the States with them Vincent?" I asked.

"No, I'll need to go back to London for a few weeks to finish up with the project I'm working on. Are you going to the airport?"

"No, Lecia and I thought it would be best to say our goodbyes here." Miles had returned with his backpack.

"Mijo, I want you to be good, and I'll call you and Mami tonight. I love you forever and ever."

"I'll miss you Daddy, and I'll take care of Mami until you come home." I took him into my arms, hugging him as if it was the last time, I would see him; and Lecia joined us in an embrace.

"We'll meet you downstairs," Vincent told her as he encouraged his kids to say goodbye before he ushered them and Miles out the door. "Goodbye Uncle Cade."

"Goodbye kids." Then it felt as if something heavy had slammed into my chest, as it was Miles's turn to say goodbye.

"Au revoir Daddy."

"Au revoir Miles." I waved as he got into the elevator and he turned and waved back at me.

"I'll meet you all downstairs," Lecia informed them and the elevator door closed.

"Are you sure you don't want me to go to the airport with the two of you?"

"No Cade, I think it will be better for all of us if we said our goodbyes here. It's going to be a long flight, and I don't want Miles to cry after we take off. The kids will be a good distraction for him—for both of us—and I'll be counting the minutes until you return to us. I draw strength in knowing our love will get us through this." I pressed my forehead to hers and took her into my arms one final time.

"Well, I guess the time to say so long is here. I won't tell you goodbye Lecia. We'll be back together soon. Never forget how much I love you and Mijo."

"I couldn't forget if I wanted to. My heart won't let me." We kissed one last time before I walked her to the elevator. She entered the car and threw me a final kiss. I caught it and pounded my chest before throwing a kiss to her as the elevator door closed. My feet were too heavy to get me back in the apartment with haste. I looked around, wishing something would come to mind to distract me from the pain of loneliness. It amazed me how quickly that feared monster of the heart could plague a soul. I got back inside the quiet space that had been filled with laughter for the past few days and I closed the door. The doorbell rang again, and I went to open the door. It was Vincent again.

"Somebody left something?"

"No, I was in your shoes for the first-time years ago and I know how difficult the first few days can be."

"Do you want to go out to a bar?"

"No, but the idea of a drink right now may be what I need to dull this pain. I'm feeling like shit right now." My phone buzzed in my pocket and I pulled it out to open the message. There was a picture of Lecia and Miles smiling at me with the caption, "Never forget we love you."

"I love you two." I spoke to the picture as if expecting it to respond.

"Brother let me fix you a drink. Scotch?"

"Yes and make it a double."

# CHAPTER FOUR

*Two months later in Paris.*

"Cade, didn't your assistant tell you I called and to call me back immediately?"

"Whoa bro." Vincent was loud and there was a hard edginess in his voice.

"I got your message Vincent, but I was on the phone with Lecia and Miles when you called. By the time I got off the phone, I could hear the frenzied yells of the crowd calling me to the stage and the energy of the crowd was fantastic. I don't normally keep my fans waiting, but I must admit, the anticipation of hitting the stage amid that kind of pent-up demand was a rush. Lecia and Miles were alright, and they said everything was good with the family, so what's going on?"

"Lecia doesn't tell you everything when she knows you're about to hit the stage does she?"

"Well no, but I know my wife and there was nothing unusual in the sound of her voice." I was becoming terse and direct under his interrogation.

"She may not know what's going on then," he continued.

"What the hell is going on? You still haven't told me, and do you expect me to play twenty questions with you? Bro, that's not your style, and it's starting to get irritating. It's three in the morning my time and I'm not in the mood for games."

"Let me get to the point before I get on the next plane to bust your ass. I'm looking out for you and your family Cade." He was silent for a moment and the delay wasn't helping my mood.

"First, Miles and Lecia are staying with my family. They've been here for about a week."

"She told me Miles and Aria are hanging out with each other. I didn't know why they had to stay at your place instead of with the folks, but I'm guessing you're about to tell me."

"You know I built a man cave for myself because of my long hours when I'm trying to finish a project. Well, Miles has slowly moved down into the space, claiming it as his bedroom."

"Was Lecia okay with this? And why have you allowed it if it's a problem?"

"Let me finish Cade." I ran my hand through my hair. I was tired and in no mood to solve another problem in which my family overindulges my son, my wife is irritated by the indulgence, and I'm the bad guy who must put Miles in check.

"Your son told me the house was too quiet at night and he was used to going to sleep hearing you, playing your horn or practicing your music on the guitar. He couldn't sleep without music, but it was a disruption for the others since my kids were used to going to sleep in a quiet house. I knew he was missing you, so I indulged him by letting him stay in my man cave listening to your music while I worked next door in my study." *There goes that word again, indulgence.*

"It was working out alright at first. He slept well and woke up in such a good mood. That son of yours has talent. He sings and dances better than the other kids. He has that *it,* factor."

"Vincent, I'm sure you're not calling me because you want to manage Miles's talent, are you?"

"Cade, I went to get Miles to take him to bed, and I discovered him creating little fireballs with his hands. I thought I was going to shit my pants. I couldn't believe what I was observing." I listened, initially in shock or disbelief. I didn't know which, but I couldn't help throwing back my head in laughter.

"Bro' you got to get off the drugs. I know you work hard, but I think it's starting to get to you."

"You know I don't do drugs."

"Then is it the alcohol? Should we blame it on the alcohol?" I responded, laughing.

"Listen, Cade, either you're concerned about your son or you're not. I'm not kidding; I'm really concerned about this." I tightened my lips in anger and this time I remained silent as I measured my response.

"Vincent, we don't need to waste time hitting each other's buttons. This must be serious, or you wouldn't have called." He let out a long breath as his frustration traveled through the line and into my ears.

"I'm damn scared if the truth be known. Miles had turned on the fireplace without my permission, placed rows of his soldiers in front of it, and was throwing fireballs from one flank of his toy soldiers to the other, as if simulating a battle. He was so engrossed in his play he didn't realize I had entered the room. I asked him what he was doing and told him playing with fire was dangerous. He told me he only played his game in that room because the floor and walls were made of stone and wouldn't easily burn. He told me he knew how to operate the fireplace and only turned it on when I was downstairs with him. I asked him to show me how he created the fireballs and he did. Little fireballs came out of his hands when he focused his attention on them. I've contacted experts at the Network who've done some research on this and they advised me that I shouldn't tell anyone other than you and Lecia since his powers place him at great risk for kidnapping by terrorist groups who could use his skills for evil intent. They also advised that we should take him to the Institute of Health in Maryland to have him examined. There is a team of doctors working with patients with various manifestations of this condition. It seems the cause is mainly genetic."

I was trying to process what I was hearing and said nothing in response.

"Cade, are you still there?"

"Yeah, I'm just trying to wrap my head around this. You're telling me my son, Mijo, is some freak who can create fire with his hands and you're concerned he could burn your house down? You moved him in with your family because of this and placed them in danger too?"

"No, I moved him and Lecia here because she was getting caught in the battle of wills between our parents and her parents. They wanted her to start alternating her time between her stay with our parents and them. Of course you know Miles was spending more time with our family if you count how many times Lecia tried to accommodate our mother and grandmother. I took Miles and the twins on a camping trip, and since that time Miles and Lecia have been here with us. I think Lecia was relieved to get out of the middle of the conflicts and she tried, but it was becoming impossible to please both sides and that's not the worst of it."

"Spill it. I can't imagine it could get worse."

"You know Miles keeps a little notebook?"

"Yeah, I gave it to him to record new words or little poems he was composing."

"He left the notebook when he went to visit the Tavares family and I discovered it. The notebook fell out of my hands and I opened it to the page labeled revenge," he snarled. "I guessed it was one of his new words, but directly under it was the name Mario."

My breath was getting shorter and my skin was hot. My vision narrowed and the room around me looked like a blur.

"You're telling me…you're telling me that Miles had Mario's name in his notebook. Why?"

"I asked him, and he told me Lecia was reading to him when her phone rang, and he saw the name Mario come up on the screen. He said she answered it and told him to stop calling her. He said she was sad and told him not to worry when he asked her about it. He knows his mother and he was worried she was acting differently, I guess distracted for several days. He said he was going to use his powers to make sure Mario never upset Lecia again. I think Mario has continued to call because she was jumpy when the phone rang yesterday. I called you to let you know what was happening and to ask how you wanted me to handle this." I got up, went to the closet, and started throwing things in a suitcase as fast as I could.

"Cade, are you listening to me? You didn't answer my question."

"What question? I'm trying to gather my things and I'll need to contact my assistant to let him know about the change in my schedule. I have a week off, but I may need more time."

"I asked if you wanted me to tell Lecia we had talked, and you were coming? The jet is on the way to pick you up and the crew will notify you after they land."

I pondered my options and decided on my course of action.

"Don't tell her I'm coming. If she's trying to protect me by not telling me Mario has been calling her then I need the element of surprise on my side. I promised that bastard I would kill him if he contacted my family and I guess he needs to find out I'm a man of my word."

"Cade don't do anything rash. A security team has been activated and will meet you at the airport. You and Lecia can decide upon a course of action once you get back to North Carolina."

I sat on the bed trying to gain control of my emotions.

"I guess I should be glad they are in North Carolina instead of alone in New York. Does Lecia know you're aware that Mario has been contacting her?"

"No, I don't think so, but I'm concerned she may have her own plans to apprehend him. She doesn't need to use herself as bait to lure him out of hiding. He's no dummy and my guess is, he hasn't evaded capture without help from others, like members of his family, who have a relationship with her family. I decided against confronting her directly because I didn't want her to decide to leave my home if she felt I was prying in her business. Your wife doesn't like other people making decisions for her."

"Tell me about it. I need to make some phone calls and finish packing. I'll get back with you as soon as I can. Bye."

# CHAPTER FIVE

Between the thoughts racing through my head, the turbulence on the plane and the meeting of the minds with my security team, I may have gotten two hours sleep max.

"I don't want my wife, or my child used as bait to flush Mario out of his hiding place, but we're going to get the bastard by any other means necessary. He's probably in town wanting a reunion with Lecia," I reminded my team as we disembarked from the plane and walked toward the limo waiting for us on the tarmac.

"Cade, whatever you decide, promise me you won't go after Mario alone," my security chief, Paul Brennan added as he made sure his gun was secured in the holster.

"Me and the guys are going to stay in the pool house at your brother's place, and I have guys stationed at the perimeter of the property just in case that fool tries to come to her. I would suggest you make sure Lecia and Miles don't go to her parents' house, at least for the next few days, since he may have someone casing their place. There is also a strong possibility his mother has been helping him remain in hiding."

"I believe that's true too. I'll do my best to keep Lecia at the estate, but my wife is headstrong and doesn't like being told what to do once her mind is made up."

I looked out the window and saw my reflection in the dark glass. I looked like I could use a good shave, a hot shower and a warm bed, but it was clear I needed to put those creature comforts on hold until we came up with a plan to keep my family safe and make Mario pay for all the pain, he has caused us. I looked around at how much the city had changed as we rode down the BG Parkway on our way home. Charlotte was no longer the small, sleepy southern town of my youth. It was now a sleek, bustling metropolis. Despite the chic apartment I had in New York or the adventures of traveling throughout the world spreading love through my music, this was where I was born and had begun my journey on this planet. *I guess it's true, there's no place like home and if you're lucky, you'll feel welcomed every time you go back.*

I took my phone out of my pocket and placed a call to my brother.

"Hi, it's me. We're in Charlotte on the way to your house."

"Hey. I'm glad you're on your way. Lecia's phone rang at the breakfast table this morning and she was so nervous after she looked at the screen, I thought she was going to pass out. Miles looked at her over his glass of milk and asked, Mami is that Mario again? Is that why you look so sad? I thought she was going to disappear into the floor. Dana dropped the plate of food she was serving to the kids and Lecia said nothing at first. There was no way she was going to start a conversation with Miles that led to her telling him he was mistaken, and Mario had never called her. That kid doesn't lie and doesn't stand for anyone calling him a liar, so she just said she wasn't feeling good and excused herself. Dana and I felt it was Mario. Miles slammed his little fists on the table and said he was going to use his powers to punish Mario. We both know about his powers bro."

"Vincent, I'm not convinced you weren't seeing Miles mastering a magic trick. The kid is bright, and I wouldn't be surprised if what you saw was a sleight of hand."

"We can't afford to be in denial about this Cade. You'll see it for yourself."

"Can you stall Lecia if she wants to leave until I get there?" He took a breath and his response was delayed.

"Sure, I can do that. While I have you on the phone, I need to ask you to do me a favor."

"What is it?"

"Our mother is barely speaking to me right now. She's still pissed I moved Lecia and Miles out of their home. I tried to explain my actions to her and Dad and I even shared my concerns about their safety with Mario lurking around, but Mom insisted they were just as safe at their house. I told Dad about Miles and his thing with fire, but I don't want to share my concerns about Miles's powers with Mom until we have him assessed. Barbaro got involved since she didn't feel as comfortable coming to my house to visit with the children any time of the day and night as she does at Mom's and now, she's mad with me too."

"You called our grandmother Barbaro. It must be bad because we both know how Barbara Olivia can be."

"It's that bad. She reminded me she would always love me, but she didn't like my take-charge manner. That's unless it benefits her and helps her to get something she wants."

"That's true. So has Mom stopped helping Lecia and Dana with homeschooling Aria and Miles?"

"No, she's angry, but our mother would never be vindictive, especially when it came to the children. She's Lovely Lauren with Dana, Lecia, and the kids, but with me, I keep my distance, so she won't be tempted to hiss and scratch me with her claws. She'd listen to you if you told her you agreed with my actions. She's always had a soft spot for her Kaiden. Doris and I have watched you over the years twist her around your fingers, baby boy."

"I appreciate all you've done, and I'll make it right between you, Mom, and Barbaro, I promise. The traffic isn't too bad, and I should be there shortly. See you soon."

"You can't get here fast enough brother."

"Bye Vincent." I ended the call and laughed as I imagined the great Vincent shuddering under the threat of our slight in stature matriarch, Barbara Olivia Rogers.

"This place is sprawling. It looks great." I leaned my head out of the limo to get a better look at my brother's estate.

"You haven't seen it since we completed it, have you?" Vincent met us at the guard station and got in the car to direct us around the back of the property so that I could get in the house with less likelihood of being seen by the family until after our talk.

"No, I left on my tour of Europe just before you all left New York and moved back to North Carolina."

"Oh yeah, that's right. You know I'm ready to help you and Lecia design your home on the property the folks have deeded to you. Your son has a love of architecture, and if I hadn't seen him dancing and heard him singing, I would have encouraged him to be an architect or maybe an engineer. He has the aptitude for it, but I think he's got a different calling. Grammy Mommie thinks he's destined to be an entertainer."

"I'm not sure if I want my son to be in the business, but it's his decision."

"Pull up right here next to my car," he told the driver, who drove up alongside one of Vincent's luxury cars and stopped at the back of his home. I looked around his home, with its manicured lawn and gardens, pool, and private entry.

"We can enter in through my office suite while the guys get comfortable in the pool house. Let me know if you all need anything." He got out of the car and directed my personal security chief and his assistant to the pool house behind the manor, then pointed toward the entry into his home.

"I spend a lot of time down here when I'm at home working on a project. The suite of rooms down here all have thickened walls and are soundproof, which is great when I want to listen to music on full volume or when I need to talk to the Network."

"It's dope down here man." I looked around at the rooms with some of the walls made of exposed brick, granite floors and niches carved in the walls made of marble. "So this is where you and my son like to hang out. I see why you moved him here since you're concerned about him possibly starting a fire. There's lots of stone around here."

"Yes, I like the look and feel of stone. There's not a lot of flammable materials in this area of the house, and I have a sprinkler system installed throughout the home." He motioned for me to be quiet as we got closer to a room with the sound of my son's voice coming out of it. He stopped at a doorway and we both leaned inside. To my horror, Miles was kneeling on the floor, trying to put out a fire with his toy soldiers burning before him.

"Oh, Mami and Uncle Vincent are going to be mad at me and Pops will make us come back to Paris." He furiously patted the burning toys with water-soaked towels in both hands.

"Miles, what are you doing?" I flew into the room and grabbed the towels out of his hands to put out the fire. I moved him out of the way while Vincent and I contained the flames. It didn't take much effort to put out the flames, and Miles looked at me, eyes wide and mouth opened in surprise. We contained the fire and I looked directly at him.

"You're not going to give your daddy a hug?" He flew into my arms and hugged me as tight as he could.

"Pops what are you doing here? You didn't tell me you were coming home."

"No, I didn't tell you, but it looks like I got here just in time. What are you doing? Haven't we told you it's dangerous to play with fire? And what's this thing with calling me Pops?" I pulled him away so that I could look into his eyes.

"I wasn't playing Pops, I mean Daddy. I was planning how I was going to take care of Mario."

"Tell me how you planned to take care of Mario." I looked at Vincent and he nodded. We both needed to understand the nature of Miles's plans.

"I'll show you." He grabbed one of his larger action figures and placed it in front of us. I couldn't have imagined what was about to unfold before us as he extended his small arms and pointed his fingers toward the figure, emitting a fireball that consumed it.

"What the—" I couldn't believe it. "Miles stop it." He placed his hands on his thighs while Vincent put out the flames.

"I told you the kid could produce fire." I grabbed one of Miles's hands and Vincent grabbed the other for a closer examination.

"Miles be honest with Daddy. Is this one of your magic tricks?" I searched his eyes for the answer. He had never lied to me and I wasn't about to tolerate it now that the stakes were higher.

"No Daddy. I just know how to make fire. I've been doing it for a while now. You want me to show you again? I can produce a lot of fire and I plan to use it on Mario. See?" He extended his hands again and Vincent batted them to the floor.

"Whoa buddy. We believe you can produce fire, and besides, this stone cost me a lot of money. I don't want burn marks that I'll have to pay to have removed on my floor." He furrowed his brows.

"Sorry, Uncle Vincent. I don't want you to be mad at me. I only want Mario to feel bad about what I'm going to do to him." I turned his head to me.

"Do you know who Mario is and what he looks like?"

"No, I only know he's a bad man who makes Mami sad." We looked up and Aria was running into the room.

Vincent rolled his eyes and muttered under his breath, "Things are getting a little complicated right now."

"Uncle Cade!" she shrieked and ran to me to embrace me.

"Hi, Aria, my pretty girl. I can't believe how you've grown. You've gotten taller." I kissed and hugged her back.

"Are you home for good? We missed you."

Vincent grabbed her before I had a chance to answer.

"Were you looking for me or for Miles?" She looked up at her father.

"Daddy, I was looking for Miles. Mommy and Tia Lecia bought some ice cream, and since we all did our chores, they told us we could have a little ice cream and then go out and play. Come on Miles." She got up and took his hand.

"Wait a minute," Vincent and I spoke in unison. He looked to me to take the lead.

"I was planning a surprise for Lecia." They both looked at me and giggled.

"What kind of surprise?" They opened their mouths and waited to hear about it.

"I'm the surprise. She said she missed me, and I wanted to come and make her happy."

"You'll make her happy Pops."

"Miles, you're calling me Pops again. Why the change?" He looked at me then at Aria.

"I live in a house with four people calling Uncle Vincent Daddy all day long and when I call you Daddy, they all get confused. Even Aunt Dana asked who I was talking about. She said I sound so much like Austin, she thinks it's him talking about his daddy, so that's why I call you Pops. It's less confusing around here. Uncle Vincent is the Daddy here."

"I understand your logic, but it's going to take me a minute to get used to the name. I liked being your daddy." I looked at Vincent smiling at the children. *I need to reclaim my place in my family.*

"I know you're my daddy. I'll just call you Pops. I also have to remind Senora Lydia you're my daddy." I cocked my head to the side, unsure of where he was going with this.

"Why is that so?"

"She always grabs my cheeks and tells me I'm handsome like her son Marco. She told me he should have been my daddy. Then I tell her Cade Moore is my daddy. Pops, she's mean and very ratched."

"Yes, I've heard her say that too and I didn't like it." Aria corroborated the story and patted him on the shoulder.

"I think you meant the word *wretched*, Miles," Vincent corrected him.

"No he's right. She's ratched. That's what they say about a hot mess or ugly person on Hip-hop Love. We watch it with Alex and Lexie all the time." She covered her mouth and raised her eyebrows.

"Oh, oh, I spilled the secret. Are you going to be mad at Alex? Daddy, he'll be mad with me if he knows I told you." Her eyes filled with tears and he reached to take her back in his arms.

"I won't say anything for now but the two of you have to promise not to tell anyone that Uncle Cade is here until after he surprises Aunt Lecia. Can I depend on my big girl—and you too Miles—to keep our secret?"

"We won't tell. We promise. Right Miles?" Aria nudged him with her elbow.

"Ouch. I won't tell." Miles rubbed his arm and frowned at Aria.

"Aria and Miles, where are the two of you? Are you down there?" Dana called from the top of the stairs.

"They're down here with me Dana. I'll send them up now."

"I didn't know you had come back home. I should have known they were down there with you. There is no one else who could keep Aria from enjoying a cup of ice cream. Don't take too long you two."

"We're coming." They giggled, and Aria placed her index finger to her closed lips to encourage Miles to keep the secret while Vincent and I began pushing them to the door.

"Remember Miles, it's a secret." I gave him a final word to encourage his silence.

"But Pops, I have one more thing to tell you."

"Can it wait Miles? If you stay down here much longer your mother or Aunt Dana will come down here looking for you and the secret will be out."

"But Pops…." Aria grabbed his hand and pulled him to the door. "Come on Miles, we have to go, now." He looked back and I pushed him forward.

"Go Miles. We'll talk more later." I let out a breath as they walked out the door.

"We've got a problem and I'm angry with myself that I've had my head up my ass for so long chasing the next professional success and good reviews that I've not been there for Lecia or Miles. I've let my priorities get out of whack."

"We're family and when one of us has a problem, all of us have a problem. We'll solve this together, but we must prioritize our course of action. I'm here for you and willing to follow your lead." Vincent looked to me for direction as I rubbed the stubble on my chin and looked absently around the room.

"I want to focus on Miles and get him the help he needs more than I want revenge on Mario. He's going to get what's coming to him. It's just a matter of time."

"Alright, so you're going to talk with Lecia about this first? Do you think she knows he can produce fire?"

"I know she's concerned about his fascination with fire, and she had to let go of multiple caretakers while we were in Paris because she believed they weren't monitoring him and allowed him to play with matches, but I think that's the extent of her knowledge, and she doesn't think he has a condition. Let me talk with her, then you can share what you discovered in researching others who have the ability to produce fire."

"I don't think we should depend on Aria and Miles to keep the secret of your return from their mothers."

"I agree. Let's go upstairs and I can surprise Lecia."

"Bro, I have a bathroom down here. Don't you have some clothes in the carrying bag I think you left in the car? I don't mean to insult you, but you could use a shave and shower before you surprise Lecia. What do you think?"

"You're probably right. I could use a shower, and after I talk to Lecia, I'm going to hit the bed. I haven't slept more than two hours in the last thirty-six. I came off the stage and took your phone call after the performance. I've been going nonstop since then and I could use some rest. I'll handle this better with a clearer head."

"The bathroom is over there, and I'll go get your bag while our kids are stuffing their mouths with ice cream."

"Thanks Vincent."

"No problem. I'll be in my study when you're ready to go upstairs."

58

# CHAPTER SIX

"Hey babe. What are you doing?"

Vincent and I walked into the modern kitchen, filled with chrome fixtures and appliances and marble-topped islands wide enough to accommodate preparations for large family gatherings. Dana was seated at the large kitchen table in front of a picturesque bay window overlooking the back of the estate. I looked out and saw Alex and Austin playing basketball and the girls were bouncing up and down on the trampoline, but Miles and Lecia were nowhere to be found. Dana looked up from her laptop and squealed.

"Cade! When did you get in town? Lecia didn't tell me you were coming home?" I went over to the table and gave her a kiss on the cheek.

"Lecia didn't know I was coming. By the way, where is she?" I canvassed the room and looked out the window and found no answers to where Miles and Lecia had gone.

"Babe, is there any more ice cream left?" Vincent asked.

"Yes, it's in the freezer babe." She pointed to the door of the freezer and turned back to me.

"You just missed Lecia and Miles."

"What do you mean just missed them? If they're not here, where did they go?"

"They went to visit with her parents. I think they were having a get together for the family." Vincent got the container of ice cream out of the freezer and was about to get two bowls out of the cabinet.

"Want some bro?"

"No thank you." My mind was reeling as I thought of the possibility of Lecia and Miles encountering Mario.

"Cade don't worry about it. We have surveillance teams here, at our parents' and her parents' homes, at the Rodriguez home and at Marco's home. We've got it covered. There's no way Mario can ambush Lecia." I sighed in relief and sat down at the table. Dana placed her hand on my arm.

"It's been difficult knowing Mario is still out there, but Lecia has been strong throughout all of this. We'll survive this as a family."

"I know we will as adults Dana, but I'm concerned about the toll it will take on my little boy. He didn't ask for this mess and he deserves to be just another kid."

"Miles isn't your typical kid, and he's got a strength that belies his age. His intellect and love of words amazes me, but you're right. He needs the love, support and protection that all kids need and deserve." Vincent was enjoying his ice cream and Dana turned her attention to her children, playing in the backyard. My heart ached as I wondered if Miles was as carefree as my nieces and nephews seemed to be. *Who in the hell am I kidding? Of course he isn't.*

I pulled out my phone and texted a message to my security chief.

**Cade:** Meet me at the back with the car. Going to Lecia's parents' house to get my wife and son. Alert the team we're coming; and they should be armed and ready in the event we encounter Mario.

"I gotta go get Lecia and Miles."

"Do you want me to come along?" Vincent finished his ice cream and wiped his mouth with a napkin.

"Cade, you look tired from your travels. Why don't you take a nap and I'll wake you as soon as Lecia and Miles get back?" I could see the concern in Dana's eyes.

"Nah, I won't rest comfortably until I see them and know they're safe. I plan to come back here and catch some sleep. Don't worry about me. I'm alright. Please don't call her, Dana, and alert her I'm in town. I don't want her to inadvertently let Mario know I'm in town if he tries to contact her again."

"I'll help any way I can. The three of you are welcome to stay here as long as you want to."

"Thanks for the offer Dana, but I'd better talk to Lecia about it before I make any long-term plans. We'll talk more when we get back. See you in a little bit." I got up from the table after I received the text, and the car was ready to take me to the Tavares's home.

"See you Cade. We're here for you," they reminded me. I waved to the kids playing before I got in the car and rode off. My chief was in the back waiting to confer with me.

"We're strapped Cade, as usual, and I've been informed that Lecia and Miles arrived safely and there hasn't been any unusual activity at the home. I don't think you'll need to be armed with a concealed weapon, but it's your call."

"No, I don't think I need to take a weapon into their home either, and I don't plan to be there too long."

"Cade, you may be there a little longer than you want to. A few friends and family members have gathered under a tent in the backyard. There seems to be a celebration of some sort going on." I rolled my eyes and slumped into my seat.

"I'll play it by ear. I'm not in the mood for a party right now. I just need my family and to get some rest." I closed my eyes and dozed off for the remainder of the ride across town. The steady motion of the car riding down the streets and the calm of music piped into the back was what I needed to relax and to take a quick nap.

The car came to a stop and I blinked to bring my surroundings into focus.

"We're here Cade." I stretched and yawned out loud.

"Thanks Chief. Stay here and pray I'm not in there too long." I got out of the car and made my way up the Tavares's driveway filled with cars. I looked back across the street and saluted a member of my security team, parked in a car with dark tinted windows, maintaining surveillance of the property. I was about to ring the doorbell when I noted the door had been left ajar and Lecia, her parents, Miles and Senora Lydia were all standing in the room. My smile vanished as I stood at the door and overheard the conversation, but my presence was blocked by the wall along the flight of stairs.

"Papi, what are you doing? I don't want you to spank Miles." I went further into the room and listened to Lecia talking to her father.

"I'm not going to hurt him, but he's my grandson and I will discipline him. He can't and will not disrespect me or any adult in this home. I don't know what you're teaching him at the Moores' but I won't tolerate it here." Miles was silent and not being hit so I decided to let this play out while I continued listening.

"I'm his mother and I'll discipline my son as I see fit, Papi. You disrespect me by not telling me what he did to deserve a spanking." Lecia was locked in this face-to-face confrontation while Miles squirmed under the grip of his hand. Her phone rang, and she quickly silenced it before placing it back in her pocket.

"I'll tell you what he said, Lecia. He called me mean and ratched in front of your father and I'll tell you I was offended." Marisela came out of the kitchen and stood beside Lecia as Lydia shared her side of the story.

"What's going on here Aridio? Let that child go to his mother. You're scaring him." Papi loosened his grip and I decided it was time to come out of the shadows. Lecia looked at me, her mouth opened in surprise at seeing me standing in the room.

"Cade." Papi saw me and called out my name and I had everyone's attention in the room. I turned away from Papi to confront Lydia.

"Senora Lydia, did you also tell his Papi you pinched his cheeks, which he doesn't like, and you have continually dishonored me by telling my son that Marco, your son, should be his father?" She lowered her head, unwilling to look me in the eyes while Miles remained in Lecia's embrace with his arms placed around her waist.

"Lydia, is this true?" Papi frowned, his tone angry and determined to get at the truth. "Answer me Lydia?"

"The boy exaggerates, and his father has misunderstood my intent." She answered and crossed her arms.

Marisela came forward and placed her hands on her hips. "What was your intent? Dime, por favor. Tell me please, share it with all of us. You've said little things I haven't liked to Lecia over the years and I've told her it's because time has robbed you of everything you once had; and she has those things you covet. My Lecia is beautiful and she's smart and you've always been jealous of her." Marissa came in as the two women fumed at each other.

"El sobrino, come with me. I have treats for us in the kitchen. Hola Cade. I didn't know you were coming to

Mami's fiesta de cumpleanos." Marissa came and kissed me on the cheek.

"Pops, Abuela's birthday is today," Miles told me. "Did you say I can have a treat now, Tia Marissa?"

"Si, you can have it right now. Come." They left us in the room to discuss what felt like an old argument. *Why me? Why now when I'm so tired?* I rubbed my forehead before I spoke.

"Feliz cumpleanos Marisela but—"

"Gracias Cade, but I'm still waiting for Lydia to answer me." She held up the large spoon in her hand. "Aridio, you have tolerated this woman for years and I know she's the widow of your best friend, but enough is enough. She will not disrespect me or my children anymore." Lydia frowned and cocked her head.

"Did you ever wonder why he tolerated me years after my husband died? It wasn't just because my husband was his best friend." Senora Lydia asked at her own peril I might add.

"Papi, end this right now if you haven't talked to Mami about Mario. For goodness sakes, it's her birthday." Papi placed his hands on the sides of his face.

"You don't have to confess Ari. I already know you slept with la picara, the hussy, and she's convinced you that you may be Mario's father." Papi found a chair and sat down.

"Marisela, we have company and we probably shouldn't discuss this right now." He tried to deflect from the thunderstorm of anger heading his way and threatening to knock him over.

"Ari, it's not like it's a secret, and the rest of the family is out back under the tent stuffing their faces and drinking your alcohol." She delayed saying more to listen to the sound of people singing.

"Listen to them singing. You can hear Miles leading them in song. They're fine. Your sister Maria told me your secret before we got married and I was angry with her, but we've made peace with each other over the years. Your mother came to me and spoke with me about you and Lydia before she died. She was a good woman, bless her soul." She made the sign of the cross before continuing.

"My own sister betrayed me?" He puffed up his chest.

*Might as well express your own anger and indignation when cornered.* I looked as Papi tried hard to maintain some control over the situation disintegrating in front of him.

"She was honest when you weren't, and your mother didn't believe Mario was a Tavares. She said he had the sign of the Rodriguez family—you know it Lydia, the second toe longer than his big toe. Don't Marco and Mario both have that sign? And they look so much like their father and uncles? Wouldn't you say that Lydia?"

"I won't let you call me la picara. I'm not a hussy. I thought we were friends."

"We were. Now get out of my house Lydia."

"I never thought you would treat me like this Marisela. We've known one another since we were girls in the Dominican Republic and we're going to end our friendship like this?"

"If you knew me like you say you do, then you would know not to mess with my children. Goodbye Lydia. Grab your things and go now before I forget we were once friends." Senora Lydia brushed by me on the way to the door and turned back once more before she left.

"You've changed Marisela, now that you and Ari have money and Lecia has married a rich and famous man. Me nor my children are good enough for you anymore." *Why am I being pulled into this drama?*

"Marco is a good man, and I've loved him since he was born. He'll always be welcomed in my home." Marisela would not be dissuaded.

"And no love for Mario?" Senora Lydia looked at Marisela and back at Aridio. "I take it by your silence Ari that you're alright with this. I'll leave, but remember you had a role in the man Mario became. He always knew you favored Lecia, Marco, and even the memories of your dead son Miguel over him. I'm gone." She walked to the door and slammed it behind her.

"Lecia can we leave? I'm really tired and I wasn't prepared to attend a party." She said nothing, so I pled my case with her mother.

"Marisela, can we celebrate your birthday later? I promise to come back and maybe we can all spend the day together."

"I'll go get Miles and I'll be back. I understand, Cade, why you don't want to stay here any longer." Marisela came forward and patted me on the shoulder while I sat down succumbing to fatigue.

"Mami, please, it's your birthday." She hugged her mother who patted her on the back.

"Don't worry about it mija. We can celebrate it later." She loosened Lecia's embrace and headed to the kitchen door.

"Wait Marisela," Papi rubbed his cheek and spoke to her in a subdued tone.

She paused to listen to Aridio as she faced the door and took her time turning to face her husband.

"I must ask you this before you leave. If you knew all about my past with Lydia, why didn't you say something sooner?" She let out a breath before she spoke.

"I guess that would be my sin Aridio. I didn't tell you because at first, I wanted you to suffer with anxiety wondering if your secret would be revealed. I thought you deserved it, then as the years went by and you proved your faithfulness to me and our family, it didn't matter as much anymore, and I didn't want to open old wounds. Instead, we allowed those wounds to fester in another generation, and look at where it has gotten us. It needed to stop, and I refuse to let this hurt Miles any more than it already has. I'll go get our grandson."

Marisela left, and I didn't try to break the uncomfortable silence between Lecia and her father who both sat in their chairs unwilling to look at each other.

I rose from my chair after Marisela returned with Miles, loaded down with food and presents. He went directly to Papi instead of his mother or me.

"I'm sorry if I disrespected you Papi in your own house. I won't do it again and I don't want you to be mad with me or Mami." He took Miles in his arms and sat him on his lap.

"Your apology is accepted, but only if you accept my apology. You reminded me today that I should have listened to you because there are always at least two sides to any story and only one truth that may be hard to accept. I know you've heard Senora Lydia say things about your parents and you defended them today. For that I'm proud of you. I focused only on teaching you to respect others, and I forgot respect must be earned and not taken for granted. I'm proud to be your grandfather even when I feel I have to discipline you."

"Your apology is accepted Papi." He grinned and hugged him. Marisela gave Lecia her purse and took the apron Lecia was wearing from her.

"Lecia and Cade, I must apologize for not supporting the decisions you've made in raising your child. I know you've decided as parents to refrain from spanking him, and even though it's not my way, I must, and I will, support your decision. He's your boy and you have the right to raise him as you see fit. I hope we'll be able to get past the mistakes of today as a family."

"I accept your apology Aridio." I went to him and extended my hands. I also got my son, so we could leave.

"We'll be alright Papi. I accept your apology." Lecia turned to her mother and hugged her but made no attempt to show her father affection.

"I'll call you later Mami," she walked toward me and Miles standing near the door. She never left without hugging her father unless they were angry with one another.

"Adios, Mami, Papi," she said and took Miles by the hand.

"Adios." I echoed, and with that we were gone and, on our way, back home.

The car was waiting for us in the front of the house and my security chief got out of the car and spoke into the miniature phone around his wrist. Immediately the occupants across the street got out of the car all clad in dark suits and shades and provided noticeable surveillance of the area as we walked to the car. Some of the neighbors came out of their homes while others pulled back the blinds and peered out of their windows.

"Is everything alright with the family Lecia?" A neighbor waved and yelled across the street.

"Hi Mr. Wilson, everything is fine. Nice seeing you again," Lecia responded as I hurried them to the car. Miles moved along as if this was a natural occurrence since he had spent most of the six years of his life under armed protection. This was his normal in New York and Europe—and now here in North Carolina. No, it wasn't the carefree childhood I had envisioned for him, but I wasn't about to take any chances with his safety. We got in the car and Lecia started immediately with the questions as we pulled away from the curb. Her phone rang again but she didn't answer and instead took it out of her pocket and threw it with force into her purse.

"Do you need to take that?" I frowned, knowing it was probably Mario.

"No I don't, and do you think this show of force is necessary? This is a very safe neighborhood." I didn't miss that she was trying to distract me, but I didn't want a conflict to mar our reunion either.

"Is that how you greet your husband who's come all the way from Paris to surprise you?"

"Kiss him Mami. You know he wants a kiss from you." She pursed her lips and opened them with urgings from my tongue, which I placed in her mouth after blocking Miles's view of us.

"Why didn't you tell me you were coming here Cade?"

Miles piped up. "I knew he was home. I saw him in the house before we left." Miles pulled a big cookie out of the bag and began munching on it and dropping crumbs all over the back seat.

"Why didn't you tell me your father was home?" He bit into the cookie again and answered her with a mouth of gooey chocolate chips swirling in his mouth.

"He told me not to. It was a surprise and he was the surprise."

"Miles, don't you think you've had enough sweets for one day? Tia Maria made a cupcake especially for you, you had ice cream earlier, and now you're eating a cookie."

"Abuela said it was her birthday and I could eat anything I wanted. She said that made her happy. I'm just trying to make everybody happy."

"Why didn't you tell me you were going to visit Abuela and Papi, Mijo?"

"I tried to Pops, but you wouldn't let me. You kept saying go before Mami or Aunt Dana come looking for you and Aria."

"I did say that didn't I." Lecia reached over a grabbed a tissue out of the side pocket on the door.

"Come here Miles. Let's eat the rest of the cookie later and I'll wipe your mouth and hands before you leave chocolate stains on the seat." She leaned over me, grabbed his head, and started wiping his mouth.

"You feel a little warm to my touch. Do you feel alright?"

"I feel a little funny Mami, but I'm alright." He was on my right and Lecia was seated on my left.

"Come and let me hold my family so we can all feel a little better." Miles snuggled into my arms.

"You're right Lecia. I think he's running a fever," I told her as she settled into my arms on the other side. She stroked my chest and looked at me.

"I'm sorry you had to witness that hot mess back at the house. Not the best way to welcome anyone back home, is it? I'm sure you wished you hadn't come to join us. What did you call it Miles?"

"Call what?"

"A hot mess, an ugly situation."

"Oh that's what I called ratched."

"I think that's a good way to describe it, ratched." Lecia laughed.

"No regrets Lecia. I just wanted to come, get my family and then have us settled under one roof, but I'm getting tired. I think I need to take a nap." I yawned. "Excuse me."

"Pops, I have to make a confession." Miles patted my chest.

"A confession you say? I'm listening."

"I was making fire earlier because I was sad and angry." Lecia leaned up and looked at him.

"Miles, what did I say about playing with fire?"

"Lecia, the boy is confessing. Let him talk." He sighed and continued.

"I was angry at Mario." I squeezed Lecia's shoulders and shook my head, hoping she would not interrupt him. "And, I was sad because Aria, Austin, Alex, and Lexie had their daddy and I didn't have mine." I readjusted my weight, feeling a little uncomfortable, but I needed to hear him.

"I missed you Pops, and I was sad I didn't have you. I wanted us to be a family again." I cleared my throat and pulled my son closer to me. Lecia took my arm from around her, leaving me free to cradle Miles in my lap.

"You never lost me Mijo. I'll always be there for you and your mother. I think you both needed me today and I was here for you." I looked between the two of them and they laughed.

"I think it was an understatement to say we needed you today Cade."

"We needed you today Pops. I would have really been in trouble if I'd told Senora Lydia, I was planning to kill her son." I flinched as the jolt of reality hit me that my young son could speak of murder as casually as a discussion about a video game.

*Note to self: No more violent video games for Miles.*

"Miles, you can't go around thinking it's alright to hurt someone even if they've done something to hurt you. You're better than he is, and we've raised you with love that we want you to spread to others. Do you understand?" He settled into my lap and played with the buttons on my shirt while Lecia spoke to him.

"Miles, it's not alright to say bad things to people. I understood you were trying to defend me and your father, but don't resort to saying bad things. You tell me or your father if you're being bullied or threatened and we'll handle it as adults."

"Yes Mami, I won't say bad things, but I don't want her to say bad things to me either."

"That's fair, if you understand you can't control other people's behavior, nor should you let them continue to influence your behavior. Senora Lydia is no longer Abuela's friend and she shouldn't be a problem for you any longer."

"I get it Mami. We should love people and not hate them even if they do bad things or we're no better than them."

"You've been listening to us. I'm glad to hear you understand what we're trying to teach you."

He got out of my lap and began looking out of the window and smiling.

"What are you thinking Miles?"

"I'm thinking how happy I am having us all together today. I want us to go on picnics, play basketball, make cookies and play music together. I missed all of that when we left Paris."

"So you're telling me you want to come back to Paris with me?"

"No Pops, I'm telling you I want you to stay with us so me and Mami won't have to miss you so much. I love everyone in our family, but it's not the same without you. Are you finished working in Paris yet?"

"I have to take care of some things while I'm here, but we'll talk more about my job later."

I pressed my hand to the shirt on his back and it was damp with sweat.

"Lecia, was Miles exposed to someone with a cold perhaps? He is feeling warmer." She reached over and touched his back and then turned him around and touched his forehead.

"I'll give him some Tylenol as soon as we get home."

We rode home the few remaining miles in silence. I had a lot to talk to Lecia about, which included addressing the issue of Mario.

"Cade wake up, we're back at the house." Lecia nudged my shoulder.

"What, what? You said we're back at the house?" I shook the fog out of my head and yawned.

"Can you help me with Miles? He's asleep and I need help getting him out of the car."

"I'll carry him upstairs and then I think I'm going to take a nap." I stretched my limbs and finished gathering my bearings.

"You both look beat. After you get him back to his room, I'll take his temperature and give him some Tylenol."

"Mami, are we home?" Miles stirred from sleep.

"Yes sweetheart. Daddy is going to take you upstairs and then I'll help you to bed. You'll probably feel better in the morning." I got out of the car and reached in to take him out.

"You're getting heavier Mijo." I hoisted him on my shoulder and followed Lecia into the house and up to his room. A few lights were left on, but Vincent and his family weren't at home.

I struggled under the weight of his body on my shoulder and climbed the stairs leading to his room, which had a kid-sized bed in the middle of the floor surrounded with pictures of us as a family located on his desk, his bookshelf, and on the nightstand closest to his bed.

"Did you know he has been sneaking out of his room and sleeping in Vincent's man cave?"

"Yes, and I purchased the sleeping bag that he took downstairs, so he could pretend the two of you were camping out together. He really missed you Cade, and if being downstairs pretending to camp out with you gave him comfort, I couldn't deny him that." I placed him on top of the comforter and Lecia went to the bathroom to grab a few washcloths soaked in water at room temperature to wipe the sweat off his body.

"Can you take his clothes off while I go to our room to get some Tylenol for him?"

"Sure. Wake up little buddy." He offered no resistance as I took off his clothes and shoes.

"I'm tired Daddy—I mean Pops. I love you."

"I love you more." I hoped I was giving him some cooling relief by taking off his clothes. He began to shiver, and I grabbed his robe, slung across a chair nearby, just as Lecia was walking through the door with the medication and a small glass of water.

"I'll take it from here. Why don't you go get some rest and I'll take care of Miles? Maybe we can talk a little, or better yet, wait until tomorrow to talk." She offered Miles the meds and gave him a sip of water.

"That's a good boy," she offered him some encouragement and he fell back on the bed.

"I'll be there shortly Cade. You should get some rest." Miles had closed his eyes again and was asleep before I could give him a goodnight kiss.

"Feel better Mijo." I backed away and left Lecia tending to our son and humming to him as she had done so many nights before when he was a sweet baby boy.

*Man, this has been a day,* I thought, reflecting on recent events. I was glad it was over, and I peeled off my clothes as fast as I could. I threw them on the floor too tired to fold them neatly as I knew Lecia preferred. I had invaded her comfortable space and had no idea how I would tell her I wanted her to return to Paris with me. We may have been far away from family in Paris, but this controlled chaos living with family was too much. I plopped on the bed with the confidence I would figure things out after I got some sleep.

# CHAPTER SEVEN

Do; do,do,do,do,do. ♫

"What the hell is that? Can't a man get any sleep around here?"

I yelled into the darkness and looked around the room to orient myself. I looked at the clock beside the bed and saw I'd been asleep for about an hour and that I was in bed at my brother's house. I heard water coming from the bathroom and dim light framed the closed door of the room where Lecia had probably gone to take a shower.

Do; do,do,do,do,do. ♫

The melodic sound of a cell phone filled the room again, and I turned my head to the sound, coming from Lecia's purse on top of her dresser. I pulled back the covers after the fog in my head settled and went to retrieve the phone.

*This could be the break I was looking for.* The air was cool in the room and I only had on my boxers. Lecia never kept it this cool in the bedroom when we lived in Paris—and I never went through her pocketbook either. I shrugged as I rationalized, I needed to get to her phone as fast as possible and stop Mario from tormenting her. I opened the bag and the phone was on top with the name Mario lit up. I placed my hand on the phone and before I could press the accept call icon, Lecia grabbed it out of my hand.

I turned and faced her dressed in only a terry-cloth robe as darts of anger were shot at me and droplets of water flung from her hair sprinkled my face as she tossed her head from side to side and assaulted my ears with an angry tirade of Spanish words. I don't know when I stopped focusing on her mouth, but I directed my energies back on getting the phone out of her hand before it stopped ringing. She backed away from me toward the bed and I followed her, reaching for her hand, but for goodness sake, I couldn't loosen her grip on the phone.

"Cade, let me go!" She fell back on the bed and I fell beside her, still trying to get the phone out of her death grip. We rolled the length of the bed and fell on the floor with my body on the bottom to brace her fall. At that point I decided if I couldn't get the phone out of her hand, I would at least try to press the accept call button. Her phone continued to illuminate the room casting shadows of our bodies in a physical struggle on the walls.

"Lecia. Let. Me. Have. The phone." The carpet was damp and sticky from the water flung from her freshly shampooed hair mixed with the sweat we had worked up while tussling with each other. The sweat on her hand was what I needed to finally loosen her grip and wrestle the phone away from her. I pressed the accept call button and Lecia stared at me motionless as I mouthed to her, *Say something.* Not a sound came from the other end as the seconds on the phone call continued to mount, followed by a call ended message. I was out of breath and so was Lecia as we lay on the floor trying to avoid eye contact. I wasn't sure what to say to her or if she would listen if I tried. She was breathless and angrier than I'd ever seen her, but I was relieved when she began speaking to me. Silence in Lecia's possession was a deadly weapon.

"Cade, you have violated so many boundaries, including the blind trust I have in you. I—"

The door opened, and we turned to see our son standing in the doorway wobbling as he struggled to walk to us.

"What are you doing? Are you playing with each other? Mami I don't feel well." He swayed as he drew closer to us before collapsing on the floor.

"Cade call 9-1-1. We need to get him to the hospital." I located her phone on the floor and called an ambulance for assistance while Lecia rushed to Miles's limp body on the floor. I grabbed my pants and Lecia screamed.

"Dios Mio, help me. Cade, Miles is having a seizure. He's still very hot."

Vincent and Dana had come into the room and gathered around Miles, whose eyes had rolled to the back of his head, teeth clenched tightly, and he was frothing at the mouth. His arms and legs began to shake uncontrollably followed by a sudden stillness and him staring into space.

"Miles. Miles, it's Mami. I'm here baby."

"Vincent, can you make sure security knows the ambulance is on the way while I stay here with Miles to let Lecia and Cade get dressed? They need to be ready to go in the ambulance with him." Dana yelled orders to Vincent.

"Sure Dana, I can do that." Dana took control of the situation as Lecia cradled Miles in her arms.

"Lecia, you and Cade get dressed. I'll be right here watching your baby. He's not having another seizure and I won't leave him. Please, the ambulance should be here shortly."

I helped Lecia to her feet and directed her to the walk-in closet to put on some clothes as we prepared for transport to the hospital. Her hands shook, and her chest was heaving, but she shed no tears as she grabbed her clothes and shoes.

"Cade, what have we done? Here we are fighting over Mario, the phone, and things that are not as important as our child. I should have stayed in the room with him."

"Lecia, let's get dressed so we won't delay the EMTs transporting him to the hospital." I grabbed my shirt and shoes while she got dressed in the closet before quickly returning to Miles. The EMT personnel arrived and placed him on a stretcher to take him to the hospital. The children were lining the walls outside of our bedroom and the three younger ones were crying as we passed on our way outside to the waiting ambulance.

"We'll call you when we have some news from his doctors. Call the other family members and tell them not to worry. We'll be in contact as soon as possible." I held on to Lecia's hand as we rushed downstairs.

"Doctor, isn't it unusual that he hasn't spoken a word to us in three days?"

"Yes, Mr. and Mrs. Moore, it is quite odd that he still hasn't spoken. He hasn't had a seizure since his initial seizure, and the brain waves on his EEG returned to normal after his first day in the hospital. I've called in a professional on his case and we're awaiting the results of his consultation, but again the good news is that his fever is gone, he's been seizure free for the past three days and his vital signs have remained stable."

"Thank you, Doctor." Lecia and I continued to hold hands as the doctor left us to maintain our vigil around the clock at Miles's bedside, still disturbed by the fact that he wasn't speaking to us and had remained minimally responsive for days. The family members had come to support us, but Lecia always seemed more relaxed after a visit from my grandmother, who was due to come back for a visit this morning.

"Good morning everyone." Grammie Mommy came into the room with her bag of healing ointments and oils with Aria walking behind her.

"I told Aria I was coming to work on Miles this morning and she insisted that she needed to come with me. She even refused to study her lessons if I didn't bring her and she reminded me she had her papers to assist her cousin."

"Hi Tia Lecia and Uncle Cade." She came in and hugged us before returning to Grammie Mommy's side to assist her in laying out the oils.

"Hi Miles, it's me and Grammie Mommy. We've come to pray over you."

"Lecia, I know you're a woman of science, but I've always believed that when science and faith collide at just the right point and time, an eruption of healing occurs like a miraculous explosion." She said a prayer over our son and began spreading oils on his body. Aria assisted in loosening the caps on the bottle for her since her joints were swollen from arthritis.

"You're a good little helper Aria. I'm glad you came to help me."

"Of course, Grammie Mommy. We help each other because we love each other."

Miles remained motionless except for his eyes and the slight movement of his head, which followed his great-grandmother's and Aria's soothing voices, reminding him how much they loved him.

"Miles, I need you to do me a favor." He turned his head slightly in her direction and fixed his eyes on her. "Your doctors think you can't talk. I need you to tell me your name and my name, so you'll be prepared to answer their questions when they come back to see you." She pointed to herself first.

"What's my name?"

His lips moved, and he whispered her name. "Grammie Mommy." Lecia and I laughed with delight and kissed his cheeks.

"What's my name?" Aria came from behind her grandmother and pointed to herself.

"NeNe."

"No Miles, I'm Marie Ariadne but you call me Aria."

"No, you're NeNe," he said again in a voice slightly above a whisper.

"Miles, who are we?" I pointed to myself and his mother.

"Mami and Pops." A slight smile spread across his face for the first time in days.

"It's alright if he calls me NeNe. We have a friend named Robert and we call him Bob, and our friend Elizabeth, we call her Lizzie, and then there's Malik and we call him Leek, so I can be NeNe. You know who Malik is, Grammie Mommy. He's Miss Hannah's grandson."

"Yes, yes." My grandmother nodded. "Hannah is a lovely woman and she has a wonderful family." She answered Aria before turning her attention back to Miles.

"What is your name?" She asked Miles.

"Miles Moore."

"Correct, and I baptized all my babies, so I should know their names, right?"

He looked at her with a blank look on his face and added nothing to the conversation, although Aria stood beside her nodding her head.

"This little girl's name is Ariadne or Aria."

"Her name is NeNe." Miles had the same stubborn streak I had, and I hoped my grandmother didn't see this as the moment to bridle his determination to call Aria by this new name.

"Alright, we'll talk more about this later."

"Grammie Mommy, she's my NeNe and I love her very much." He pointed to Aria.

"Alright my sweet baby. Who am I to interfere with the spirit that has delivered you back to us?" She gave the bottles to Aria to replace the caps.

"I love you too Miles," she told him as she began helping Grammie gather her oils and ointments back into her bag.

"I don't want to hear that you're not eating your food, and tomorrow, if I get good reports that you're eating your meals, I'll bring you a special treat to celebrate that you're getting better and coming home soon."

"Thank you, Grammie Mommy." He looked at her and smiled.

"Yes, thank you Grammie. I can't tell you how much comfort you've brought to me over the years. You are a woman of great faith, and I do believe in the skills of modern medicine and the prayers of a fervent woman." Lecia hugged my grandmother.

"I know you do and together we have been a powerful force for good. Get some rest and I'll see the three of you tomorrow."

Grammie hugged each of us and gave Aria a kiss on the cheek.

"You've been a wonderful helper Aria, uh…NeNe." She laughed and grabbed her great-grandmother's cane.

"You said, Grammie, that there can be no love without sacrifice. I'll be NeNe for as long as Miles needs me to be, but I need to get home, so I can go to Austin's game tonight. I promised I would watch him play. He needs me too."

"Yes sweetheart, you are blessed to be needed and loved. I promised your parents I'd get you home in time."

"There's a special plan for that boy's life Cade." Grammie pointed a finger at Miles.

"I believe you Grams, and thanks again." I breathed a sigh of relief that my grandmother always had enough faith for all of us.

Settling in for the night, Lecia and I were placing sheets on the pull-out bed when Miles spoke spontaneously to us for the first time in days.

"Mami. I'm hungry." She rushed to his bedside.

"I placed your dinner in the refrigerator sweetheart. Will you eat something if I warm it up?"

"Yes Mami. I want something to eat."

"Daddy will stay here with you while I get your food, alright?" She stroked his hair and kissed his forehead before going to the kitchenette near the nurses' station.

"I'm here for you Miles, and I'm glad you're going to try to eat something. It will help you get your strength back."

"I want to be strong like you Pops. I need my strength to do my list."

I looked around to make sure no one was in earshot and, leaning over him, I whispered into his ear.

"Buddy, let's not mention the list again alright? Especially not to your Mami."

He nodded but I knew his list was never too far from his mind.

# CHAPTER EIGHT

"So how did it go today?" I returned to the hospital from a long day of rehearsal with the band after Lecia insisted I leave our vigil at Miles's bedside. He had remained afebrile and seizure free, but we hadn't seen a return of the active, rambunctious child we'd adored before his seizure. I kissed them both and found a chair to hear the report of Miles's fifth day in the hospital.

"Well, he went to play therapy and physical therapy today and the reports from both therapists were that he was making progress, slowly but surely. Afterwards, he had lots of visitors from both our families. He had a good appetite for breakfast and lunch," she told me as she kept her hands busy folding clothes and tidying the room.

"Mami can I have some more pie?" Miles looked up from his drawing on the bedside tray, filled with paper and tons of colored pencils and crayons.

"Miles, I told you we need to save what's left of the pie for later. You've already had two pieces and that's more than enough." She smiled at him. "I haven't forgotten that Abuela slipped you a cookie while I went to check on your meds at the nurses' station. You were wearing the crumbs around your mouth when I returned."

"Lecia, Miles has had a tough time lately, and the kid even had to spend his eighth birthday here in the hospital. Are you sure he can't have another piece? You know Grammie Mommy makes the best sweet potato pies in the world. They are worth the sugar overdose. Where is the pie?"

"Cade, you're not helping matters any, and the pie is in the kitchenette. Grammie came earlier today and left two pies. I think the nurses ate the first pie and Miles is trying to eat the second pie by himself."

"What? You weren't planning on sharing some of the pie with me Miles-y?" I got up from the chair and ran my hand through his hair and pushed him lightly on the shoulder, which ignited return punches from him on my chest and giggles.

"Please be careful Cade. He still has an IV in his hand."

"Mami doesn't like when we play like horses Pops."

"It's called horseplay Miles, and we shouldn't let the fun get out of hand."

"You didn't like it when Pops was horse playing with you and you were rolling on the floor with him?" We both stopped what we were doing and looked at him directly.

"You remember that Miles? I placed my hands on his shoulders and looked into his eyes. I wondered if the image of me and his mother rolling on the ground frightened him.

"Yes, I remember. It happened on the night I got sick. It looked like fun and I was coming to join in, but I fell, and that's all I remember. Mami, can I please have some more pie?" We both let out a breath. We hadn't exactly been fighting each other that night, but the physical encounter had escalated to a level that neither of us wanted it to go.

"Maybe later Miles and please stop asking about the pie." Lecia was firm in her response to him.

"Yes, maybe later Miles-y," I added in support.

"Pops, stop calling me Miles-y. I'm not a baby anymore and I don't want a baby's name." He lowered his head and began drawing on the paper again.

"Pops can you bring my notebook to me? I left it at the house." I gave him a quick sideways glance and he whispered, "I said notebook, not my list."

"Miles, maybe your Dad can get you a new notebook that has a hard, leather-bound cover on it as one of your birthday gifts. I'm impressed with how you have kept up with your notebook, and your new special notebook could be just for your new words and the poems you like to write. Did you tell your Pops how you used your new words passion, ignite, desire and transpire to come up with a new poem?"

He handed a piece of paper to me to look at his poem. I knew my wife and her Supermom hearing had probably heard Miles mention the list to me. I looked at his poem and tried to steer the conversation away from the list by reading his poem aloud.

"My love is afire,
you ignite my desires,
magic transpires
when I'm with you,
when it's just us two."

"Did you copy this from somewhere?"

"No Pops, it just came to me while I was listening to your music."

"This is mature writing for someone so young. I was writing about trucks, balls, and airplanes at your age, not about love."

"He spent most of his eight years of life surrounded by adults and he's writing about things he's exposed to Cade. He has written a little more about footballs and basketballs since we came back to North Carolina." Her phone buzzed in her pocketbook, catching our attention, including Miles's.

"Aren't you going to answer it Lecia?" I raised my eyebrow as I questioned her.

"No, it can go to voicemail. Did I tell you that Grammie Mommy came for a visit this morning?" She fidgeted with the fashion magazine she had picked up and was pretending to read.

"Yes, you did. Remember, you told me she brought two pies."

"Yes, yes. So, I did, but I didn't tell you how she lovingly sliced a piece of it and fed it to Miles one spoonful after another even though I encouraged him to feed himself. She kissed him after every two or three spoonfuls of pie and would have given him another large piece if I hadn't stopped the two of them. I'm glad to see his appetite has returned, but it's not wise to overly indulge him, and all the sugar he has consumed today isn't good for him either."

"Pops, do you want to see my picture?" He handed it to me and I looked at the simple drawing of a heart colored in red with the word "imagination" written below it.

"It's a heart and I would have thought the word love would have come to mind."

"Imagination is my new word. I told my therapist I planned to have more money than my grandfathers, my uncle, and my Pops so that I would never have to leave the people I love, and he told me I had a great imagination. Love is not complicated Pops. You stay with the people you love because you don't want them to be sad."

*Hell, what do I say to that?*

"Miles, I've told you that adults have to work; and we can't always be with the people we love." She looked up from the magazine she was reading as she spoke to him.

*Great save Lecia.* Miles looked at her with one of his blank stares, which often meant he didn't buy it, but he wasn't going to argue the point.

*I guess it's my turn to offer an explanation.* I took my time approaching the delicate subject.

"Miles, I know our separation has been difficult, but you've got to know how much I love you and Mami and how important you are to me. I have to work, and I've been blessed to find a career that gives me immense pleasure and the ability to earn a decent living for our family. I have to leave, but I'll always come back to you."

The nurse came in with his medication and he took it with a small cup of juice.

"Miles don't forget to tell your grandmother thank you for the pie she left us. It was the best, ever."

"I will." Lecia gave a small eye roll as the nurse exited the room. "Pops go get the pie, so you can taste it before it disappears. I told you it was good."

"Enough Miles Moore. I told you 'No.' You have a large vocabulary and I know you understand the simple words no and stop. Stop it and stop it now." Lecia closed the magazine and placed it on the nightstand beside her.

I couldn't imagine that what happened next would change our lives forever.

"Mami, you don't let me have any fun." He pushed the hospital tray away and papers flung throughout the room after the tray crashed against the wall causing a loud thump. His chest started heaving and he began hissing at Lecia, who sat on the couch wide-eyed and mouth gaped in disbelief.

"Miles! I said stop it." Lecia stood up, screeching at him.

Fisting the sheets to steady himself, he began rocking wildly in the bed. Then he grabbed his head and yelled, "I just wanted some pie!"

His eyes turned red and his skin flushed with color as I watched, shocked at what I was seeing. I was about to grab him when the veins in his arms became more visible and his hands burst into tiny flames that ignited and caught the bed linen on fire.

"What the—" I stopped in my tracks, my mind racing and uncertain of how to handle this shit.

"Do something Cade! The bed is on fire!" Lecia was screaming, Miles was yelling, and the door opened, turning my attention briefly away from Miles to my brother Vincent and Aria coming into the room.

"What the hell?" Vincent pushed Aria toward Lecia and looked around the room for the fire extinguisher on the wall while I threw the pitcher of water on Miles and on the bed, putting out the flames on his hands and on portions of the sheets.

"Grab him Cade while I extinguish the sheets." I grabbed him, but he continued to shake more from anger than the trembling I'd witnessed when he'd had the seizure.

"Give him to me Cade." I was hesitant but took him to his mother, who was waiting for him with one outstretched hand and the other hand comforting Aria.

"Cade help me put out this fire before the alarm—"

"Too late." I remarked. The alarm went off and the sprinkler wet all of us with sprays of water pulsing throughout the room. Several nurses came running toward us, including the charge nurse.

"What happened in here? How did the bed catch on fire? Is everyone alright?" The charge nurse looked around the room at the bed with the charred sheets and paper flung around the room as she questioned us. I answered for us, a group of wet muskrats, with guilty looks the water couldn't wash off our faces.

"We're fine and the fire is out."

"What caused the fire?" She continued to look around the room and ran to the corner to disarm the alarm on the wall and turn off the sprinkler before giving orders to the junior nurses.

"I think the electronics on the bed panel overheated and caught on fire." Vincent always said I was quick on my feet. I guess I developed the skill from years of covering for him, Doris and myself when we were growing up. The charge nurse narrowed her eyes as she shook the water off her hands and her electronic tablet.

"Alert fire safety that we have everything under control and there's no need for an evacuation. Have someone deliver towels to the room while we make plans to relocate Miles to another room. We'll also need someone from the supply department to come and look at this bed. This is quite unusual, Mr. Moore, and we've stocked these beds for the last five years without incident. I'll need to inform his doctors, so they can examine Miles. Take his vitals, Nurse Johnson, while I contact his medical team."

"Yes Ma'am." Nurse Johnson attended to her duties and took his vitals before departing with the rest of the nursing team while Lecia wrapped Miles and Aria in towels to dry their skin and clothes. He had calmed under her steady gaze and she spoke to him for the first time since the start of what would later be called, "Pie-gate."

"I'm not certain how to explain what just happened despite my training and experience, and honestly it's frightening to me, but Miles, I'm your mother, I gave birth to you, and I'll never be frightened of you. I get it you were angry with me, but I'm standing my ground with you. When I say no, I mean no. No pie, no back talk, no disrespecting me. I don't care if you can produce fire, turn into a dragon or incinerate the entire world. Do you understand?"

"Yes Mami." My jaw dropped as I looked at him relenting to her demands while she cuddled him as they sat on the couch covered with towels.

*Think. Think.* I grabbed my head as thoughts ran through my mind. *What should I do now?*

While I paced back and forth, it was Lecia who provided some understanding of what was happening.

"Cade, Dr. Martin or whoever is covering for him will be here soon I'm guessing. I've read about a rare case of a child who could create fire, but it also ran in his family. There's no evidence of it in my family. Are you or Vincent aware of this condition in your family?"

"No Lecia. I've never heard of it before." I answered.

"I'm doing some research on the family, but I haven't had a chance to complete it." Vincent looked over at Aria as he spoke.

"Are you alright Aria? You don't seem too surprised by what you saw. Did you know Miles could create fire?" She looked down and away from Vincent before answering.

"I'm ok and yes, Daddy I knew. I'm sorry I didn't tell you or Tia Lecia."

"Don't be mad at NeNe, Uncle Vincent. I made her promise not to tell." The two of them looked at each other, thick as thieves, caught in one secret, but chances were, there was more to tell.

"Who is NeNe?" Vincent wrinkled his brow and looked at Miles.

"That's me, Daddy. Miles has given me a new name."

"What's wrong with the one you have?" He frowned at the two little ones.

"Bro, it's a long story and I'll share it with you later. We need to be prepared for questions from his medical team."

"Yes, you're right Cade." I turned to address my next concern with Lecia.

"Babe, can you trust me to take the lead on this?" Vincent had already contacted members of the Network, the secret society of professional operatives who rescued Miles from kidnappers when he was an infant. They were involved in his medical care and I wasn't sure how I was going to explain their role to her. I didn't want her to worry that his ability to create fire was placing him at high risk of danger again.

"Cade, we need to get Miles help before this happen again and we can't afford to wait. I don't think this is the best facility for him." Her eyes were filling with tears as she spoke.

"We're going to get him help Lecia. Don't worry." I finished my sentence just before  Dr. Martin came into the room.

"Good evening, Mr. and Mrs. Moore, everyone." We nodded and returned the doctor's greetings.

"I've just been given an interesting account of what happened, and from the looks of this room, the account probably isn't as unbelievable and inaccurate as I was thinking on my way up to the floor. First, Miles's vitals looked good and the results of his imaging studies have come back normal. I appreciated the consultation with specialists at the National Institutes of Health that you, as his parents, arranged for me to discuss issues regarding Miles's care. Normally, getting a consultation doesn't happen in a matter of hours."

I assumed it was Vincent who had made it happen and Lecia went along with it listening to the doctor in silence.

"I discussed my thoughts and Miles's current diagnoses with the team of specialists, but I told them you haven't given me a history consistent with the possibility of a rare genetic anomaly in which Miles can create fire, but I suspect from the incident today that he can."

I listened to the doctor and averted my gaze slightly as Lecia tightened her grip on Miles's shoulder. My son wouldn't lie to the doctors if asked on direct examination, and he hadn't learned the art of subtle discretion yet, so I spoke before the doctor could question him.

"Doctor, my wife and I are aware that Miles has certain proclivities that may be genetically based, and we haven't had a chance to discuss our course of action yet. I just returned from a tour overseas and my wife and son were staying with my brother. I don't believe the two of you have met. He has been doing some research on the anomaly."

"Vincent Moore." He extended his hand to the doctor.

"I'm Dr. Martin, the lead physician on your nephew's case. I've suspected for a few days that there was something different about Miles's condition because he has taken longer to recover from the seizure, he didn't speak for days, and he had unexplained brainwaves on the EEG, as if his brain was trying to recover from something more than a seizure. The events of today confirm my suspicions. Mr. and Mrs. Moore, your son's condition is beyond the scope of what we can offer at this facility, and his abilities are a safety concern for the staff and other patients. I can make some recommendations after we have a discussion regarding all the facilities and researchers who specialize in the care of patients with his condition."

"Doctor Martin, we've already begun researching our options, and we're leaning toward a transfer to the National Institute of Health in Maryland, but please let me finish discussing this with my wife." I was speaking on the fly and sensed the tension coming from Lecia as her jaw tightened, and there was no head nodding or any sign of support for what I was saying to the doctor.

"Alright then, I'll leave you to discuss the matter, and hopefully you'll have reached a decision by the morning. The plans are to move Miles to another room for tonight while we have this one cleaned."

I looked at Miles, who had fallen asleep in Lecia's arms, and Aria was pressed against Lecia's shoulder, stroking his arms.

"Aria, I'd better get you home and out of those wet clothes. Tell your aunt and uncle goodbye." Vincent had a knack for knowing when it was time to leave. Lecia leaned into Aria's kiss goodbye and said goodbye to Vincent on their way out the door. I turned to face her after they left.

"Research Cade? You and Vincent started researching Miles's condition and you couldn't find the time to discuss it with me, his mother?" We kept our voices low to avoid waking him.

"I found out about it after I came back to North Carolina, and that's when Vincent shared his concerns with me. When did I have time to talk to you about this Lecia?"

"We've been here at the hospital for five days. Could you have talked to me then, or have you been too interested in trying to catch Mario?"

"Lecia, let's not go there, not now." The orderlies came in with a new bed and transported Miles to his new room for tonight, averting another heated discussion.

She said very little to me as we prepared for another night on a pull-out bed at the hospital. I closed my eyes to catch a little sleep before our talk and then with members of the treatment team in the morning. We both had agreed to sleep on it.

"Lecia, your phone is buzzing."

"Let's just get some rest Cade. It's been a long day." The phone stopped, but minutes later, it started buzzing again and the heat of irritation began coursing through my body. I threw off the covers and she spoke again before I got out of the bed.

"No, please let me." She grabbed her phone at the side of the bed and looked at the text on the screen before handing it to me.

"Here Cade, take it. I can't do this anymore. You and Mario have both been headstrong all your lives and now you're obsessed with making him pay for his crimes and I get it."

I looked at the text. It was from Mario.

Meet me at my apartment across from the city park on Beatties Ford Road. I know Cade has an album signing at noon tomorrow. Will text you the address before then so come alone.

I got up and didn't bother to turn on the lights as I searched for my clothes. Lecia was saying something, but she only had half of my attention. Her mouth was moving, and I heard her voice, but it kept breaking up in my ears no matter how much I tried to pay attention.

*Blah, blah, blah, blah, blah.* I stopped and tried my best to tune her in.

"I'm tired of trying to keep the two of you apart. He continues to call me despite the number of times I've changed my number, and I don't think you'll stop pursuing him until he's dead. It would have been nice if you believed the things you've told Miles about seeking revenge and being better than those who hurt you, but it doesn't seem to matter to you that you'll have blood on your hands." She was crying as I tightened my belt and slipped on my shoes.

"I think I know what apartment complex he's talking about and I'm going to put it under surveillance. I promised Mario what I would do if he tried to contact you and I'm sorry Lecia, but I'm a man of my word. Do you want me to turn him in, to bring him to justice and have Miles becomes a part of a media circus?"

"You know that's not what I want." She sat up in bed.

"Well then, excuse me. I have something I have to do."

I slipped her phone in my pocket and left her crying as she climbed into the bed with our son.

"Blessed Virgin be with us." She muttered and made the sign of the cross. I stood in reverence of Lecia's faith, which kept her strong no matter what troubles she had to face; and I looked back at her one final time before slipping out the door.

98

# CHAPTER NINE

It was in the dark of night when we drove past the popular park filled with hundreds of trees and located not too far from an old apartment complex. It was inhabited by a motley crew that included those who had fallen on hard times and were attempting to regain their dignity and place in society: felons on parole and folks who were still working the mean streets of Charlotte. Those that had yet to be gentrified.

I alerted my security team and had them place the property under surveillance before I arrived, escorted by two additional men including my chief, Paul Brennan who kicked down the door to Mario's apartment.

"Stay here. I got this. It's personal." I pointed to the team with me to stay outside.

"Cade, are you sure?" My chief asked.

"Yes." I needed them to stay outside as I walked into the room.

"Well if it isn't the talented Kaiden Moore. What took you so long?" Mario stood beside his bed and greeted me despite my lack of an invitation.

"Mr. Rodriguez, I would have come sooner if you had called me personally. Please excuse the time of my visit in the wee hours of the morning, but you summoned me by calling my wife and it was an offer I couldn't refuse."

The room was dirty and littered with old cigarette butts, beer cans, empty bottles of cheap liquor, and empty wrappers from cookies and chips. Clothes were strewn throughout the main area of the efficiency apartment which held a bed, an odd assortment of tables made of particleboard with chipped laminate covering, and a small bathroom located adjacent to the central space. The room, filled with offensive smells, reeked of smoke from the lit cigarette in an ashtray on his bed, from alcohol, body odor, and the perfume probably left by the woman coming out of the room just as I'd pulled into the parking lot.

He looked bad, but I wasn't prepared for the sight of the man who, without question, wasn't an example of integrity but at least he used to take a lot of pride in his appearance. He smiled at me, showing his dingy teeth and I noticed that his hair had thinned over the years.

"You didn't bring anyone with you? Were you afraid they would see that a punk like you could never kill me? I bet you don't even have a gun." I drew mine out of the holster before he could pull his gun out of his pocket and I fired a warning shot within inches of grazing his shoulder to get his attention. His eyes widened in shock and he grabbed his shoulder.

"I would avoid sudden movements if I were you." My security team outside the door came running into the room, after hearing gunfire.

"Put your hands in the air," my security chief barked at Mario as he moved in to frisk him. "Don't make me shoot you, but I will if you move one inch," he further instructed Mario, who continued holding his hands in the air while I watched my security guys take his weapon and hold him at gunpoint. He looked like a cornered animal standing there, and I didn't trust him.

"Mr. Rodriguez and I need to talk alone for just a little longer. You can go back outside while we finish our conversation." Mario stayed quiet until they made their exit.

"As I was saying Moore, I don't believe you came to kill me. I know my Lecia Tavares, and she would never live with a murderer. If you killed me, she would leave you. Lecia and I have too much history, and because of that I was calling so that I could apologize in person."

"Her name is Lecia Moore. Once upon of time she was a girl named Lecia Tavares, but now she is a woman, my wife, and the mother of my son. You may have known her well once, but trust me, you don't know me." I paced a little to gather my thoughts so that I could make my point as plain as I could. He looked at me as if he was going to pounce on me at any minute. I returned his stare with my own growl and baring of my teeth. On some level, I wished he would give me a reason to shoot him, but he maintained his distance.

"She probably told you that I promised not to kill you, but I never promised I wouldn't kill your mother, who by the way is a piece of work, and your brother, whom I'm not particularly fond of. My only regret would be killing your son. Is he three years old now?"

"Damn you Kaiden Moore. Damn you to hell if you hurt my son." The veins were popping in his neck and along the right side of his temple. His eyes were bloodshot, and, as my eyes had become accustomed to the dim light, I saw his skin had a yellow jaundiced tinge from years of heavy drinking and his abdomen was bloated.

"I burn with hatred for you with the heat of a thousand suns, but if it will make you feel better, kill me. Kill me right now. I dare you. But leave my family alone. What kind of man would kill a little boy? Huh?" He pointed his scrawny finger at me.

"What kind of man would steal a child from the womb of a woman he once professed to love as a sister? Please don't bore me with your examination of my moral character. You're right, I'm not going to shoot you. You're not worth the cost of one of my bullets. You're already a dead man walking but call Lecia again and I'll send every one of your relatives to the fires of hell with you."

"Fuck you Kaiden and all men like you who always get the best life has to offer and leave the scraps for everyone else. Fuck. You."

"No, fuck you and I hope you had a memorable one earlier because chances are that was your last. Goodbye Mario—forever." I backed out of the room. "Remember, I'm a man of my word, and I wouldn't do anything crazy if I were you."

I got outside the main door of the building and my brother was leaning against the hood of his car.

"Don't give me shit right now Vincent," I growled as I walked past him.

"I had no plans of doing that brother. I do know you and I know a man has to do what a man has to do, and no one has the right to terrorize your family. This was your call. I was only here as a family representative."

"Representative? Right."

"That's right, and I plan to drive you back to the hospital to be with your wife and son instead of spending hours talking to your security chief about your next move, but first we need to stop by my place, so you can wash the funk off you before getting in bed with Lecia."

"That's a good idea." I sniffed the air and Mario's funk had jumped on me.

I returned to the hospital room with a suitcase and a change of clothing. Lecia said nothing as I took off my clothes, but I knew she was probably awake because it was impossible to get one night of deep sleep in the hospital with all the monitors and people coming in and out.

I crawled in behind her and was settled into the curves of her body before she turned to kiss me.

"I brought some fresh clothes with me from the house for all of us."

"Shut up Cade and tell me you'll always come back to me."

"I promise baby. I'll always come back to you." I kissed her hard and deeply, letting our tongues and souls intertwine.

"I love you Lecia. You're my Lecia and I'll always protect you and Miles. I love you with all my soul babe." I pulled away to let her look into my eyes as the beeps of monitors pierced the silence in the room.

"I've kept my promise and I didn't kill Mario this time to avenge you, but I was willing to die for you if it came to that. I won't live with the feeling that I can't keep you safe and protect my family. I can't promise you that."

"I'll never ask you to do that Cade. You know what I can and can't live with and I know the same things about you. I love you Cade and I'll always love you no matter what happens, but I don't ever want to feel the fear I felt tonight. It pained me to think that I may have lost you forever." She started crying and I kissed away her tears.

"I'm here baby. Don't cry, I'm here." I took her in my arms and settled in for the night with my wife at my side and my son safe in the bed next to us.

104

# CHAPTER TEN

*Six weeks later*

To say that I was behind schedule in finishing my latest project would be an understatement. Instead of composing new music, I had spent as much time as I could with Miles after his discharge from the hospital, and I was looking forward to my first day of being at home alone to finish writing at least one song. We were staying at Vincent's home, and this was a rare day when Vincent and Dana planned to take all the kids, including Miles, horseback riding for most of the afternoon. Lecia had plans with her family and had left earlier this morning to help her parents at their home. I took a sip of coffee and was about to pick up my horn when Miles came running into the room.

"Miles what are you doing here?"

"Pleeease Pops. Say I can go."

"I thought you went riding with your cousins? Hey, hit that note again. Pleeease." I chuckled. "It might be the note I'm looking for."

He rolled his eyes and I picked up the horn to accompany him.

"Pleeease Pops."

I blew out a few notes as he rolled his eyes again.

"I didn't want to go so they left me." He had the house phone in his hand and began pressing numbers before I could intervene.

"Who are you calling?" I placed the horn on the desk.

"Hello Miss Hannah? Hold on."

He thrusted the phone in my face as I pondered my thoughts out loud. "That's not like Vincent and Dana to change plans at the last minute and not tell me."

"Pops," Miles huffed. "Miss Hannah is on the phone and she needs to talk to you. Tell her I can come to Malik's birthday party in the park. I have a present for him."

My phone buzzed, and it was Mike.

"I need to take this Miles." I accepted the call and watched as Miles started pacing in front of me while talking to Miss Hannah. Charlotte had many more inhabitants in the city than when I was a boy, and it surprised me that I knew Miss Hannah, who had babysat me for a couple of years, and she also knew Lecia and her family, as they lived in the same neighborhood.

"Hold on Miss Hannah, I'll place you on speakerphone," Miles told her.

I placed my phone to my ear and spoke to Mike while trying to ignore Miles's mounting impatience.

"Yeah, yeah. I said I would have the song done by this afternoon and I will Mike. Stop pressing me man. I know it's important to meet deadlines. Bye."

"Cade, Cade Moore? Are you there?" Miss Hannah's voice filled the room as Miles had turned up the volume so that there was no mistaking that he wanted my attention.

"Hello Miss Hannah. This is Cade. How are you?" I smiled in the direction of the phone and then frowned at Miles. Miss Hannah was a kind, lovely woman, and I didn't want to risk directing my irritation at her.

"I'm fine Cade. Miles said he just needed to make sure that you knew he was coming to my grandson Malik—Malik Jones's birthday party at the park today. Don't worry about bringing him. It's not a problem to stop by and pick him up and take him with me." Miles looked at me awaiting my answer.

"What time is the party?" I asked her. Miss Hannah was not the safest driver, and our driver had often taken us to the park or the children's museum when she'd sat with me.

"I'm sure the party has already started. You know my family likes to have barbeques in the park and play their music. Don't worry, we have a permit at one of the shelters so there shouldn't be any problems."

"Miss Hannah, our driver took Lecia to her parents' home and I don't want to spread my team too thin, maybe some—"

"No Pops, Uncle Vincent left one of his men outside and he said he would take me. He knows where the park is, Dad." He placed the phone on the desk and clasped his hands in prayer.

"Cade, Malik would be so disappointed if Miles couldn't come to his party. He gets excited every time he hears that Miles can come over to play with him."

"Pleeease Pops. I've done all my chores, and Mami wouldn't have to take me to the park or the library tomorrow. I can go to the park today." He flashed a smile I knew was meant to manipulate me while my phone buzzed again with a message from Lecia, saying that she couldn't find her phone but that I could contact her on Marissa's phone. She planned to go shopping with her sister and mother before coming home. I was about to return her text when the phone rang again. This time it was Wolf, my drummer. I looked up and Jackson Howard, one of the new drivers and a member of Vincent's security team, came to the door.

"Cade are you still there?" Miss Hannah asked on the phone.

"Miles are you ready to go? Hello Mr. Moore. It's no problem to take him and I can stay until he's ready to go."

"I'm ready. Miss Hannah, I'm on my way." Miles was attempting to scurry out the room when I inadvertently hit the accept call button.

"Cade, this is Wolf. I'm having problems opening the file with the music you sent earlier. Can you send it again?"

"Hold on Wolf." I was starting to feel overloaded.

"Miles, come back here." I yelled at him before he escaped out the door. He turned and came back to me. I forgot I still had Miss Hannah on the phone.

"Cade, is there a problem with Miles spending time with me and my family? Wasn't I always careful when you were with me? I loved you as one of my own and I don't recall you ever having a bad time with me?" I blew out a silent breath.

"No Miss Hannah. I loved spending time with you. Miles can come to the party, but we'll need to limit his time to two hours. I'm not sure what Lecia has planned for this evening."

"Yes!" Miles yelled and pumped his fist.

"He'll be fine Cade, and we'll have him back home in about two hours. Goodbye Cade and see you soon Miles."

"Goodbye Miss Hannah." Miles joined in with me and I ended the call.

"Add the word manipulation to your list and we'll discuss it when you get back."

"Cade!" Wolf yelled over the phone. I forgot I had him on hold.

"Bye Pops." Miles hugged me and ran out the room, followed by Jackson.

"Hello Wolf. Sorry for the delay. What did you say was the problem?"

Act II: Playing with Fire

I had just finished the final note of the song when I heard a commotion outside of the office. I looked at the clock and three hours had passed since I'd last seen Miles.

"I need to speak to Mr. Moore. I need to explain what happened. Cade. Cade!" A familiar voice was yelling outside the door. After placing my guitar on the desk, I got up and hurried to the door, where several members of the team who were routinely at the guard shack were attempting to apprehend Miss Hannah. She was elderly but hadn't lost much of her strength.

"Cade, I need to explain. Please let me explain." She pleaded with them and looked at me with a fear in her eyes that made the hair on my forearm stand up. My security chief came up behind them, and it was clear something was wrong. I scanned the room before responding.

"Let her speak Paul." He waved the men away from her.

"Where's Miles? And Miss Hannah, what do you need to explain to me?" I asked her.

"Cade, we don't have time to hear her out. I came here as fast as I could after arranging coverage for Lecia and her family. Miles is missing and Lecia doesn't know about it yet."

"What!" I focused on my breathing to stop from hyperventilating. "Take me to where he was last seen. Miss Hannah, I thought he was with you?"

I didn't stay long enough for her to answer before I went down the hall to my bedroom to get my gun out of the safe. Paul came up behind me and placed his hand on my shoulder.

"Cade, I wouldn't advise that you take a gun out to the park. We have enough firepower out there now, and we secured the perimeter shortly after Miles arrived at the park. No one will get in or out of the area with him. I promise you."

"Was the party held at the same park near the apartment where Mario was staying?"

"Yes Cade. I'm afraid so, but I advise that you give Miss Hannah a few minutes of your time before she falls apart, then we can head to the park." I turned and walked back to the study where Miss Hannah was seated.

"Alright Miss Hannah. I'll listen, but you've got to stop crying. I don't want to lose precious time."

"Cade, I went to the store to get some more ice cream after we ran out and I came right back."

"Was Miles there when you got back Miss Hannah?"

"Yes, he was." I took a breath and tried to balance the two competing thoughts in my head; *Don't rattle Miss Hannah* and *I need information that will lead to Miles's return.*

"Miss Hannah, I need you to go to the part in the story when you discovered he was missing."

She placed her index finger to her mouth before she spoke.

"Yes, yes, I remember. We had just finished serving the kids hotdogs, and Miles saw a man who looked down on his luck sitting on a bench nearby. He told me his mother thought it was a good thing to feed the hungry and he wanted to take a hotdog to the man, so I let him. He sat beside him and they looked like they were enjoying a conversation."

"How did the man look Miss Hannah? Did you know him?" I asked.

"I didn't know him, but he looked a little like Jose Rodriguez, you know, Marco Rodriguez's uncle before he died. Jose had been sick, and he looked old and tired before he passed."

"You're sure that he looked like a member of the Rodriguez family?"

"Yes, like Jose, their deceased uncle. I couldn't place him at the time, but as I think about it, that's why he looked so familiar. Well, anyway, your driver brought out the present Miles had for Malik, which started a commotion. Miles had given Malik a brand-new BMX bicycle. Oh my goodness, Malik started squealing with delight and then there was a loud noise like firecrackers going off in a trash can. By the time we located the noise and settled down the kids, I looked back and Miles and the man were gone. My son and his friends started looking for Miles and calling him. You know my oldest son worked for your brother Vincent about a year ago. He's a brick mason, and he did a lot of work on this house. He contacted your brother and I think he said your brother tried to get in touch with you."

"Thank you, Miss Hannah for the information, but we have to go," my chief interrupted. "Can I get someone to take you home?"

"No, I can call a family member to come pick me up. I'm too nervous to drive back, but I needed to come to speak to Cade. I promised I would care for Miles and it was the honorable thing to do to answer your questions in person." She burst out crying and I caught her before she slid out of the chair onto the floor. I wasn't angry with her, but I had to focus my attention on finding Miles. She tried to get up and I made sure she was steady on her feet before looking at my phone, which I forgot I had placed in airplane mode after I'd gotten off the phone for the second time with Wolf.

"You can stay here until your family comes, but Miss Hannah, I need to get to the park. I know you're an honorable woman and I don't blame you for his disappearance. Paul let's go. We need to find Miles. I can't bear thinking I'll have to tell Lecia he's missing."

A text from Lecia came through after I took it off airplane mode.

> **Lecia**: My cousins from the DR just got into town. Will be home later tonight. Hope you got a lot done while we were away. Miles should be getting back from his ride soon. Love you.

Checking my phone log as I walked out the door behind Paul, I saw she hadn't tried to call me, and I made the decision to let her enjoy as much time as I could give her.

Besides, I wasn't certain I could hear her over the drumming of my heart in my chest, nor did I know if I could handle her tears. Lecia's sadness always tore into me, like the searing pain of a hot knife. I needed to spare us both that kind of pain.

My heart was in my stomach, as the route to the park was almost the same, as the route I had taken six weeks ago to settle the score with Mario.

"Are you sure it's the same park Paul?" I leaned in and spoke to Paul from the back seat.

"Yes, this is where Jackson said he took Miles. The park was on the edge of an area that was being gentrified and was quite nice, although the area leading to it was still undergoing significant renovations. I looked up at the skyline and could see the water tower that was located near the apartment where Mario was residing. We came to a stop and several black unmarked vehicles were at the perimeter point. I recognized some of the men who were part of Vincent's security detail, and I was sure the other men with dark glasses and jackets were Network agents. Vincent came out of the shadow of densely planted trees and shrubs, surrounded by men with dogs on leashes and walked toward me as I exited the car.

"Cade, why didn't you pick up the phone? I still don't understand why you insisted Miles come to the party instead of going horseback riding with us?" We frowned at each other.

"Vincent, that's not the version Miles told me. This is looking like he had a hand in some of this." I ran my hand through my hair and blew out a breath. "Are there any leads on his disappearance or knowledge of where Mario is right now?"

"The first thing we did was go to Mario's place, and he wasn't there, nor were there any signs of Miles. If he has Miles, they are still on foot and he will not get out of here without us discovering him." Jackson came running toward us waving his hand in the air. I prayed he had good news.

"Good evening Mr. Moore." He bowed his head to me before turning to Vincent.

"Good evening Mr. Moore."

"Evening Jackson. Do you have some news?" I got closer and hung my hopes that his words would lead to the return of Mijo.

"I do. I noticed that Miles had a cellphone in his backpack and I told him to keep it on, but I didn't tell him, it was so I could track him if I had to. We lost the signal, but it's coming back and he's still—at least, the phone is still in the park. I also saw his skills while he was playing with Aria—you know, his fire thing, and I told him today to use it if he didn't feel safe. I just had this feeling that something wasn't quite right, but I went back to the car to wait for him instead of keeping him under closer surveillance. I thought he would be safe at the party surrounded by the Jones family. He's a smart fellow and that little boy has no fear. I just wanted to let you know that the odds are in our favor that we'll find him."

"Good, and that tracker you placed in Mario's watch, that night he passed out after Cade's midnight rendezvous, should help us to locate Mario. Good work."

"Thank you, sir. I knew he wouldn't leave without that watch. I had intel on him and I knew the name Rafael engraved on it was his father's name. He's a piece of shit, but I guess there was a time when he loved at least one human being: his father."

"Jackson, give me your gun. I'm going to need some firepower." I extended my hand to him. I feared Mario had something to do with this, and now I was sure he did. "He needs to understand that Moore men keep their word." Jackson was about to reach for his gun when Vincent stopped him.

"You take his gun and then what will he have? The gun is registered to him and must remain in his possession. Come on Cade, you know the deal. Jackson, come with me, and Cade—stay here."

# CHAPTER ELEVEN

Several hours had passed, and the sky was clear, but dusk was settling in and more men joined in to search every inch of the park and the surrounding area. Looking up at the horizon, I tried to calm myself by gazing at the sun, which had begun to set, leaving ribbons of pink, blue and gold. A breeze was blowing through the leaves on the trees, and the sounds of little nocturnal animals scurrying in the underbrush in the park caught my attention. My sense of hearing was a gift when it came to analyzing music, but infused with fear, sounds around me were painful. The hoot of the owl caused my head to snap around to seek out where it was coming from, and trucks carrying heavy loads thundering down the streets nearby felt like an assault on my senses. I covered my ears, but it didn't mute the drumming of my heart. I looked over at my brother, who always seemed to rise to these occasions. I swore the man had ice running through his veins, but unlike Mario, my brother respected and cherished the gift of love in his life.

In my peripheral vision, I saw a member of the security team coming toward me with an article of clothing in his hand. I turned and walked toward him.

"Do you recognize this Mr. Moore?" I took the small jacket from him and turned it over.

"Yes, this belongs to my son, and see—it has his initials sewn in it." I pointed to the embroidered initials MAM. I sniffed the jacket and it smelled of smoke.

"Where did you find it?" I asked him.

"Over there, about a quarter of a mile away. It smelled of smoke but there was no evidence of a fire in the vicinity, and it didn't smell like cigarette smoke either. Don't worry Mr. Moore, we won't stop until we find Miles. I like that quirky kid. He always makes my day."

"Thanks." For the first time, I choked on my words and fought to hold back tears. The man turned and walked away, granting me some privacy as I calmed myself. I loved my quirky kid too and couldn't allow myself to think that something bad had happened to him. I looked around and neither Vincent nor Paul had returned to the parking lot, where I stayed surrounded by security cars and several men. I didn't have a gun, but I had my phone. Mijo was impulsive, but he knew how to play a situation to his advantage. I pulled out my phone and decided to text a message to Lecia's phone. Miles didn't have his own phone, and the phone Jackson saw in Miles's possession probably belonged to Lecia.

Are you okay? Talk to me.

I walked in the direction of the old apartment complex and wondered if I should walk along the path to the street where the dilapidated building stood. I could kick myself for letting Mario go. Maybe Mario had the right idea—to take no prisoners. I kicked at the fallen branches and stomped on them to release some of my anger before looking at the phone. My heart almost leaped out of my chest as I saw the little dots alerting me that a message was coming.

IOK.

I laughed so loud, releasing my tensions, that some of the men came running to me.

"Miles communicated with me. I need to let my brother know I heard from Miles." I told the men as I texted a message to Miles.

Where r u?

I stared at the phone and I didn't get a return on my text, but my phone started ringing. It was Vincent.

"Hi Cade. We got him. He was running through the woods and we located him after he started using the phone. He said he texted you back, after you contacted him."

"Yes." I tried taking deep breaths to relieve the pain settled in my chest. "Where are you? Does he look okay? Do we need to have him checked out medically?"

"He's dirty and has a few scratches on his arms, but otherwise he's fine. Cade, I'm in the car with him heading back to the house. Meet us there."

"No, bring him to me now Vincent. I need to see my son."

"Wait a minute Cade. I'll let him say something to you before I pull up the partition for some privacy. Say something to your Pops Miles."

"I'm alright Pops. I smell bad and I'm tired." I laughed, not to make light of the situation, but laughter was the easiest way to discharge my emotions, still pent up from the last several hours of looking for him.

"Alright, I'll meet you back at the house. I love you Miles."

"I love you Pops, and now I know you and Mami will be safe."

"Miles—"

"Cade not now. Let's wait. I'm raising the partition now, so I can speak candidly to you while he's in the back with one of my security guards." There was a pause as I heard the electronic hum of the window going up in the background.

"Cade, you've been triggered, and I know how wicked your temper can be when you're hyped, but I don't understand much about Miles's fire thing. He probably wouldn't do it, but I didn't want him to burn up our asses if you laid your hands on him in anger. So please take your time getting back to the house, calm down and we can talk to Miles hopefully before anyone else gets home. Enter my office suite from the back of the house and we'll be there waiting for you."

"I'm his father Vincent, and I plan to address this issue with him like any father would. He's my son and he needs to know that if he set this—no, I'm sure he set this mess into motion, and it's unacceptable. He could've been killed. I'll never fear him. He comes from me and he's a part of me."

"Do what you have to do Cade."

"I plan to Vincent."

"Alright. Adios Cade. See you at the house."

"Adios Vincent."

What Vincent didn't understand was that, in the last six weeks, Miles and I had formed an even closer bond and understanding. I'd spoken to him directly about his powers and told him that others may try to get him to use it to harm other people. I'd gone so far as to talk to him about using his power in anger against me or his mother. He'd laughed at me.

"Why would I use my powers to hurt people I love? That's silly Pops." He'd shaken his head before putting his hand into the bowl we shared and stuffing his mouth with popcorn while we watched television together.

"Mijo, you know how much me and your Mami love you, don't you?"

"Yes Pops." He rolled his eyes. "You tell me that every day. I love you. Don't I tell you that enough?" I let out a hearty laugh.

I reflected on those memories and realized that Miles knew I would never harm him or lay my hands on him; both he and Vincent were concerned about their dark shadows. On most days, Miles had my temperament, but I could also see there was part of both him and Vincent most people would never want to see. I was comforted by the thoughts that they both needed the time to get acquainted with that aspect of each of them. I had a dark side, but Vincent and I suspected Miles had an aspect of himself that was dangerous and not black—a mixture of all colors under the sun. Something dark but not sinister, like a midnight or indigo blue.

I opened the door to the limo and got out before my security guy could bring the car to a complete stop, right after we passed through the gates leading to Vincent's home. Running full speed to get to Miles, I couldn't tell which of Vincent's employees opened the door for me. I didn't stop, didn't say hello and couldn't calm myself until I approached the door of Vincent's study. I heard them talking and saw Miles seated in the chair facing Vincent. His clothes were soiled, and he nodded his head as he looked wide eyed at his uncle pointing a finger in his face.

"Don't say anything that's going to make him angrier than he already is. Do you hear me Miles?"

"Yes Uncle Vincent."

"Answer all of his questions. Just the facts." Miles was nodding as I entered the room and he looked around his uncle's imposing figure standing above him. Before I could say a word, he got up and raced into my arms.

"I'm sorry Pops. I'm really, sorry. I didn't mean to worry you." I kneeled and hugged him, breathing in his earthy smell as I kissed the side of his face and his neck. My heart was pounding hard, as if it needed to push out my stress, mixed in the pungent odor of sweat and my tears. Thoughts that I could have lost this boy surfaced and threatened to flood me with fear that only my laughter soothed.

"Why are you laughing Pops?" Miles pulled away and looked at me.

"If I wasn't laughing, I would be doing something else that isn't good." I wiped away my tears of relief and a frown immediately spread across my face. I placed both hands on his shoulders and focused my attention on my voice instead of my impulse to shake some sense into him.

"Miles, what were you thinking? Why did you take your mother's phone and I'm assuming you contacted Mario, not the other way around?" He remained silent as Vincent came and placed his hand on my shoulder.

"Bro, I know you need answers, but can you ask him one question at a time. You're not only confusing him, but I don't know where to start either."

"Alright, that's fair. Miles, have a seat." He went to the chair, where he had placed his backpack in his lap before he attempted to answer my questions.

"Pops, I just wanted to tell Mario to stop making Mami sad and not to call her anymore, and he told me he would stop, if I met with him."

"And you couldn't tell me about it, Miles?" I paced and barked at him.

"Cade, you're yelling bro. Please calm down. You'll draw Dana's or the kids' attention if they return and you're down here yelling," Vincent reminded me.

"Where's Mami, Pops?" Miles looked up at me, eyes wide. I knew he wasn't accustomed to me yelling at him, so I calmed down.

"She's at Papi and Abuela's house. I'm asking the questions here."

"Yes Pops. Mario told me I couldn't tell anyone about our meeting. He called me out Pops, and I did what any man would've done. I had to show up."

I looked at my son, now eight years old, and snarled. "So you're a man now?" He wisely chose not to answer that question.

"Did you think it was alright to lie to your Aunt Dana and Miss Hannah about your plans? And let's not forget taking your mother's phone without permission." I continued my line of questions.

"I didn't lie Pops. I sent a message using Mami's phone to Aunt Dana, who was at Grammie's house, to let them know I wasn't going horseback riding with them, and I called Miss Hannah. You were the one who told her I could come to the party, and I texted Mario who agreed to meet me in the park. He knew where it was." The heat from an awakened dragon of anger rose up in me as I recalled Miles's ambush on my time. I lunged toward him and stopped short as he recoiled in the chair. I valued that Miles was such a verbal kid, and I had to remind myself that I'd promised to never cross the line, not today or ever, by laying my hands on him in anger. I blew out a deep breath. I didn't like it, but

I had to accept a hard truth. I was being manipulated by my kid.

"I didn't directly lie, but I led you to believe something that wasn't true. That's deception Pops." Vincent rushed in front of me, blocking my view of Miles, and whispered in my ear.

"Damn, your kid is good at this Miles. Future Network material?"

"No Vincent. No." The exchange with Vincent gave me the mental break I needed to continue talking to Miles without blowing my top.

"Tell me more Miles." I placed my hands on my hips and paced away from him.

"Well Pops, I offered him a hotdog while he sat on the bench in the park, and I went with him after we distracted Miss Hannah. He said he lost his cat and I knew he was lying but I decided he needed to pay for making Mami sad. I wasn't afraid of him because I have powers. I was going to use them on him, but you know what Pops?"

"What Miles?" I turned and faced him.

"He said he was sorry and that he loved Mami." He reached into his backpack and pulled out an old hospital band for a newborn and gave it to me. I looked at it and typed on the label were the words "Baby Boy Moore, Mother-Darlene Moore." That was scratched out, and above it, "Alicia" was handwritten. I tightened my grip on it and closed my eyes.

"Can I see it Cade?" Vincent held his hand out and I placed the band in his palm. I opened my eyes and saw Miles opening that damn notebook and scratching out something.

"What are you doing Miles?" As if I didn't know.

"I'm drawing a line through Mario's name. You and Mami are safe now and she won't be sad anymore.

"Did you ever think how sad I would've been if something happened to you? You're my only child Miles, and I would've been devastated if something bad happened to you." I ran my hands through my hair and tried to swallow the lump in my throat. He looked up at me and ran into my arms.

"I didn't think about that Pops. I never wanted to make you sad. I love Mami and you. I needed to do something to protect you." He looked into my eyes.

"Miles, you're just a kid. You don't need to protect the adults. Do you have other names on your list?"

"No Pops. Grammy Mommie and I talked about forgiveness, and I erased all the other names after I understood forgiveness and grace—all the names except Mario's." We both looked over at Vincent, whose phone was buzzing. He read the message and looked at me.

"We need to talk Cade." He held up his phone and I turned my attention back to Miles.

"So why did you just scratch off Mario's name? What allowed you to finally do that?"

He didn't hesitate before answering my final question.

"Justice Pops. I finally got justice." He looked me in the eyes and didn't blink. I had never seen that look before and wasn't sure how to interpret it.

"Did you do something to him Miles? You can tell us the truth."

"No Pops. He was alive the last time I saw him. He said tell your Mami I'm sorry and he let me go."

"Go and wash, Miles, before Mami gets home and sees you like this. I'll be there to help you in a bit. You know there will be consequences for your actions, don't you?"

"I thought there would be Pops, but first hug me tight so I can feel your love." I placed my arms around him and kept him in a bear hug while placing kisses on his cheeks. He reciprocated and kissed me on the cheek before leaving the room and closing the door behind him, after which I turned to face Vincent.

"I just got the text message that a secret cell of agents has been activated by the actions of Aquila coming in contact with Andromeda. The orders for the cell are irreversible since Ganymede was also involved." His lips tightened.

"What? What are you telling me? Who's Aquila, Andromeda and the other thing?" I pursed my lips and waited for some answers.

"I can tell you now Cade that Andromeda is Lecia's code name and Ganymede is Miles's code name in The Network, since their names will be changed after the activation of this cell of agents known by the code name Killer Bees."

"Does that mean Lecia is in danger?" I tried to make my way to the door, but he blocked my exit.

"No, the signal was from Lecia's cell phone, which Miles carried to meet Mario, and was what the Killer bees responded to after it came within proximity to Mario's signal. Relax. Lecia isn't in danger, and no we didn't place a chip in your wife." He laughed at me.

"So Mario sealed his own fate?" He nodded, and I went to the bar to fix a drink. "Do you want one?"

"Sure Cade. Why not?"

"I tried to warn him that Moore men keep their word." We stood in silence as I filled his glass with vodka and handed him the drink.

"So you did brother." He grabbed the glass and looked at it.

"Here's to justice." I took a sip from my glass.

"Yes, justice." Vincent took a sip of his drink then looked up at me and smiled.

"Cade, wake up." Lecia shook my shoulder as I was sprawled across the bed asleep.

"What? What time is it?" I looked around and tried to get my bearings.

"It's very early in the morning and I just checked on Miles. He was still asleep, and he didn't move when I kissed him on the cheek. The two of you must have had a busy day." She covered her mouth to stifle a yawn.

"I'm sorry I'm getting home a lot later than I planned, but a neighbor came to Mami's and told her Mario was found in a fire in an apartment across town. I thought he was hiding out somewhere in the Caribbean since it had been over a month since he last tried to contact me. They said they found him dead."

"He was found dead?" I repeated it for emphasis and yawned while I stretched my limbs.

Lecia looked me in the eyes, and I was happy she didn't have a superpower of x-ray mental vision to detect any lie.

"I'm only going to ask you one time and then I'll never speak of it again. Did you have something to do with Mario's death?"

I looked her in the eye, without blinking, and with a relaxed posture answered her question.

"No I did not Lecia." Her eyes roamed my facial features before she responded.

"Alright, that's all I needed to know Cade."

*I'm not lying. I didn't order his execution. She had her chance to ask if I knew anything about Mario's demise, and she didn't. Outright lying is different from a little deception, and Miles begged me to not tell her of his escapade before he went to bed. I'll not share it with her, at least not now. Lecia and Miles are safe and nothing else matters.*

# CHAPTER TWELVE

"Thanks, for helping me clean up, Lecia. I wasn't expecting so many people to come pay their respects to Lydia." Marisela was busy wiping down the tables that had been placed around the room.

"Marco didn't want to have her repast after the funeral at his tia's home, although she had volunteered to host it. He wanted to do it here, and how could I refuse?" Marisela sighed.

"He said his tia and Lydia didn't get along in life and Lydia would have haunted him in death if he had agreed to let his tia host the gathering after his mother's funeral. Poor boy."

"Why am I not surprised that the two of them didn't get along?" Lecia responded and shrugged as I kept busy folding chairs.

"Lydia was a complicated woman as you well knew her to be. Cade, can you place the fold-up chairs in the corner over there? Gracias."

"No problem Marisela. Anything else I can do before we leave? We left Miles with my parents, and after four hours of watching him, I'm sure they could use a break."

"I was hoping you could stay for a glass of wine with me and Aridio. It's not like we get to see you all as often now that you've moved to Maryland to be nearer to Miles's new doctors. Please sit a while with us. Aridio will be downstairs soon. He needed a little rest after all the excitement and company we had today. Let me go check on him. I'll be right back."

"Lecia, I wasn't planning to spend the entire day here, nor was I going to let you go to the funeral services without me, but I think we've done enough. You were here to support your parents and I'll hand it to Marco that he kept a respectful distance from you. It's unfortunate what happened to his mother, but she's gone and there's nothing more you can do here."

"Cade, I appreciate how helpful you've been, but Mami and Papi want to know about Miles. We can tell them how he's progressing and have one drink before we go. What harm is there in one drink?"

"Alright Lecia. Only for you." I leaned over and kissed her on the forehead. "Where is the wine? Is it in the refrigerator?"

"Yes. You go get the wine and I'll find the glasses."

I went in the kitchen and was surprised to see Aridio sitting at the table with Marco and Marisela.

"I thought you were upstairs Aridio."

"Hola Cade. I came down through the back stairs." He rubbed his head.

"Hello Marco."

"Hello Cade." He returned my greeting and both he and Aridio looked worn out.

"I was getting the wine while Lecia found some glasses at the bar. I'll let her know you're in here in the kitchen." I turned to go get her, but she was already coming into the kitchen.

"Who are you talking to Cade? Oh, hello Marco. I didn't know you all were gathered here in the kitchen. Mami asked if we had time to have a glass of wine and I was looking for wine glasses at the bar."

"We can enjoy a glass of wine here Lecia. Come, you and Cade, sit a while. This has been a trying day for all of us." Marisela patted a chair beside her for Lecia and pointed at one for me.

"One glass won't hurt." She looked at Marco, who held his head down but looked at Lecia as she spoke to him.

"I didn't get a chance to offer my personal condolences for both me and Cade with all of the people at the funeral and here at the house."

"Yes, we're sorry for your loss." I didn't care much for the woman, but it was the right thing to say. I pulled out a chair for Lecia and then for myself. I didn't have the energy to wrangle out of an innocent enough invitation to share a bottle of wine.

"Thank you, and I appreciated the two of you being here in light of the recent history between you and my family. My mother was a complicated woman, but she loved whom she loved, and she loved them blindly. I would be lying if I said she wasn't blind to my faults, but I have no reservations in saying she loved all of you." We listened as Aridio filled our glasses.

*Yeah right.* I lowered my head and picked up my glass, ensuring my eyes were focused on the deep red wine and not rolling toward the ceiling.

"You all never asked how she died, and it wasn't until tonight that I felt comfortable talking about it."

*Now you have my attention.* Lecia and her parents looked at him as he took his first swallow of wine before he spoke.

"My brother contacted our mother and she told me she urged him to go back to the Dominican, where he has been living for the past four years."

*I knew that. Get to the part I don't know Marco.*

"She told him she was doing everything to clear his name and she planned to talk to you again, Tia Marisela, about…you know, the incident. Mario told her he didn't want her to waste her time because Lecia wasn't lying and he was guilty of what he did to her. He asked for her forgiveness and said he had tried to ask for Lecia's forgiveness. I arrived at the house right after he hung up with her, and she was in her bedroom crying when she started grabbing her chest in pain. I called the ambulance and they took her to the hospital. She was having a heart attack and seemed to be doing alright until I got the news that they found Mario dead in a fire at an old apartment complex on the other side of town. I couldn't tell her that Mario was dead and burned beyond recognition, but maybe she knew he was no longer with us because she began withering away and died a month later."

He broke down crying, and Marisela got up to comfort him by laying her arm around his shoulders and stroking his head, which he cradled in his arms on the table. I would probably never get rid of my nagging suspicions that Marco was not completely innocent of the crime, but he was clearly distraught by the passing of his mother and brother.

"Tia Marisela, how did things come to this with my family? I don't understand how my mother, who was once as good as they come, and my brother, who was my hero at one point, could both be dead and gone within a month of each other."

Marisela offered him a tissue and drew her chair close to him for comfort.

"We don't always get a tidy explanation about things that happen to us, nor do we get the good things we may deserve. It's one of the mysteries of life. Marco, your mother was complicated, and there was a time she was as good as gold. She and my mother were the ones who were there during some of the darkest days of my life. She dressed me and Lecia for Miguel's funeral. She cooked food for my table for months and she was there for me. She wasn't perfect, but no one is."

"Tia, you and Tio Aridio were there for us when Papi died, and I'll never forget it. I don't know what caused Mario to be such an angry man when he was such a loving brother to me when we were boys, but I hope there is some mercy on his soul because he wasn't all bad."

I cleared my throat and gulped down the remainder of my wine, having heard enough of the good old days. "Lecia are you ready to go?"

"Yes Cade, I'm ready." She placed her hand on top of mine and kissed me on the cheek. "Mami, before I forget, please don't bring Miles a dozen cookies and give him permission to eat them. Sugar makes him hyper and irritable and it's on his diet plan as something to eat sparingly."

Marisela pursed her lips and rolled her eyes. We'd shared the story of Pie-gate with my parents and grandmother, who'd agreed to not stuff him with sweets, but there was no telling how long they could stand the pleading of a boy who loved his grandmother's pies.

"Cade, Mario also told my mother you knew where he was for years and you could have had him arrested or taken justice into your own hands, but you didn't. I'm forever grateful to you for your mercy and sparing my mother years of grief. I know it couldn't have been easy for you—either one of you."

"Thanks Marco, for your kind words, but don't thank me. Thank Lecia. She's the one with the big heart. I hope you find comfort in knowing that the Tavares family understands the complexities of the human spirit and we have no choice but to take the bad with the good. We need to leave to go check on our son, since we've been gone most of the day."

"I too hope to see my son in the next seven months. My ex and I are expecting and have agreed to give our relationship a second chance."

Lecia went to hug her father and mother while I observed if she would hug Marco. She didn't.

"Mami, I'll call you tomorrow, alright?"

"Yes, I'll be waiting for your call mija."

I gathered our things and escorted Lecia to the waiting car. I had my security detail on full alert since I couldn't take any chances that Marco may have thought I had something to do with the deaths of his relatives and sought retribution. Lecia hadn't asked me about Mario again, but I caught her staring at me after she got the call that Mario and now Senora Lydia were dead.

"Thank you for coming with me today. I know this wasn't easy for you."

"You don't think I would have let you come alone do you?" I grabbed her hand as we made our way to the car.

"No, probably not, but you could have offered some resistance to my decision to be with my parents, to support them during this difficult time."

"Lecia, I've been married to you long enough to know that there is no changing your mind when your convictions tell you what the right thing to do is. My only concern was for your physical and emotional safety."

"I always feel loved and safe with you." She squeezed my hand.

"I plan to keep it that way, my queen." I opened the door of the car for her.

She snuggled in my arms on our way back to my parents' home and fell asleep on the ride over to the South

Park neighborhood of Charlotte, far away from the broken down, decrepit old apartment complex.

Lecia's phone started ringing and I didn't recognize the number on the Bluetooth display.

"Babe, it's your phone ringing."

"What, what is it?" She stretched and yawned. "Answer it." The driver hit the answer call icon on his steering wheel.

"Hello Mrs. Moore. You may not remember me, but I'm Joshua Holmes's mother."

"Yes, I remember you. How can I help you?" She stretched her arms.

"Well, I just wanted to make sure Miles was alright."

"Why are you asking Mrs. Holmes?" Lecia arched her brow.

"Joshua came home with bruises and blisters on his hands and he said he was in a fight with Miles, who is three years younger and smaller than Joshua. He said it was just horseplay, but I wanted to apologize and offer any assistance if he needed to see a doctor."

"I thank you for calling, but Miles is with his grandparents and they haven't called to let us know that they were concerned about an injury. Where did Joshua and Miles encounter each other?"

"My husband had Joshua and friends at a basketball game, and I think Miles went with his cousins to see Austin play today. Austin and Joshua were friends." I interrupted the conversation knowing Joshua probably received the worst end of the deal.

"Hello Mrs. Holmes. This is Miles's father, Cade, and I'm sure things will be alright. We're just arriving at my brother's home now. We do appreciate your calling."

"Sure thing. Just let me know if there is anything I can do. We have placed Joshua under punishment for hitting a smaller child. He knows we don't condone that kind of behavior."

"Goodbye Mrs. Holmes."

"Goodbye."

The car came to a stop in the driveway and Lecia hesitated before she got out.

"Cade let's just imagine how this is about to play out. Your family will minimize any role Miles played in the conflict with justifications for his actions."

"Lecia, that's not fair, especially since you don't know what happened."

"Hear me out. I know these are mere speculations, but I have history on my side for support. They will pretend to chastise Miles by giving him examples of taking the high road but also send mixed messages that he was compelled to act. Any punishment we give him will be met with resistance and undermining of our authority."

"Lecia, I can't believe I'm hearing you say *my* family overindulges Miles when you just finished giving your mother a lecture about her overdosing him with sugar. Really Lecia? You're not being impartial."

"I'm not impartial Cade. Let's go inside."

I helped her out of the car and escorted her through the back of the house and into the kitchen, where every member of my brother's family, my parents, my grandmother, and Miles was seated near my grandmother, were gathered around the kitchen table eating sweet potato pie. Well, everyone except Miles was eating pie. I looked back at

Lecia, who stood in the doorway grabbing the side of her face as if she was about to experience a monster headache just as Dana came forward to greet us.

"Lecia before you jump to conclusions please understand that I had nothing to do with this. You remember I was hosting my book club meeting today, and yes, Grammie catered it for me with her pies. Any time I tell the girls Grammie is catering the event, everyone miraculously shows up. I had some pies left over and Vincent and the kids came back from the game before I had a chance to put the pies in the refrigerator. That's all I have to say."

"How many pieces has Miles had?" Lecia looked at the guilty group.

"None Mami. You said I couldn't have any pie, remember?"

"Yes I did Mijo and I appreciate that you listened to me. Now what happened with Joshua today? I got a call from his mother."

"Lecia, you and Cade may want to have a seat. I can explain." Vincent pulled out his seat for her. "I took the kids to support Austin at his basketball game today. Lexie left early with one of the mothers from her dance group, and I had Aria and Miles. I told them to stand in front of the restroom while I used it, and when I came back, I saw Joshua hitting Miles."

"Uncle Cade and Tia Lecia, I was a witness that Joshua did hit Miles first."

"Why did Joshua hit Miles, Aria?"

"Well, Miles called him a turd, Uncle Cade."

"What is a turd, Cade?" Lecia asked me. My skin heated because I knew she wasn't going to like it.

"Mami, I called him a piece of shit. A turd is a piece of shit."

"Miles Moore!" his three grandparents said in unison.

"We don't talk like that in this house, young man. Whatever would make you say such a thing?" my father asked him, and Lecia looked up at me as if she had made her point.

"He tried to kiss Aria and she didn't want to kiss his ugly face, so he grabbed her, and I got between them and told him what I thought of him, Granddaddy."

"So you were upholding your cousin's honor?"

"Yes sir, Granddaddy." Austin and Alex came over and patted him on the back for support while Lecia looked up at me again.

"Well, there were other ways you could have made your point, but it's difficult to take the high road, especially if someone is bigger than you and hitting on you." His grandmothers nodded and Lecia sat, tapping her foot.

"He wouldn't stop hitting on me, so I grabbed his hand and I squeezed it real hard until he started screaming, 'It's hot!'"

"Well Mijo, it sounds like you had a very eventful day. Would you like at least one slice of pie?" Lecia asked him.

"Are you serious Mami? Yes, I'd like that a lot." He smiled back at her.

"One slice it is, and I think I'll have a piece too." She gave him permission as I looked at her with her arms across her chest and a smirk on her face.

"That's a good idea Lecia. I'll get a piece for you and Cade." My mother hopped up and sliced the pie.

"Thank you, Lauren." Lecia graciously accepted her pie, and while pushing a piece into my mouth, I had to concede she was right about my family dynamics when it came to Miles.

"Nothing like a piece of pie to add some sweetness to life's sorrows," my mother piped in.

"I agree Grammie," Lecia acknowledged as she watched our son swinging his legs, smiling and enjoying a piece of his Grammie Mommy's pie.

"This is so good Grammie Mommy. It makes me smile all over my body," Miles declared, and my grandmother smiled back at him, happy that her gift for baking goodies provided joy to the family that money couldn't buy.

# CHAPTER THIRTEEN

"Cade, please hurry. We're going to be late for church. You know Miles is going to lead the children's choir in a song." She took one last look in the mirror and positioned her hat on the side of her head while she listened to me.

"Every time we come down here, there's something to do. Can't we just have a visit with the family and do nothing at least one time? We relocated to Maryland one year ago for the convenience of being closer to Miles's treatment team, but sometimes I feel we're only home long enough to go to appointments, check the mail, and go to sleep before taking a plane to North Carolina. I was thinking, Lecia, why don't you and Miles join me in Stockholm for a short gig the band has there, and then after we return, we can make some decisions about continuing Miles's care in Maryland or returning here to North Carolina for good. Miles is nine years old and I'm sure he can handle life on the road. It will be fun, and we can hire a tutor to travel with us to take some of the pressure off you."

Life had been on full throttle for me this past year, after relocating to Maryland and commuting between Maryland and New York for work. I could really use some vacation time in the Outer Banks of North Carolina, for sailing and fishing with family members instead of going from one social or community obligation to another.

"Cade let's not do this right now. I can't think about long-term plans until we get through the short-term plan of letting Miles finish his treatment. Your grandmother volunteered our son for the program this morning, so let's go."

"Fine." I grabbed my wallet and headed out to the kitchen to grab a bite to eat.

"Good morning Lauren. Thanks for feeding Miles this morning. Where is he?" Lecia looked around the room and there was no Miles.

"Good morning Lecia and Cade."

"Good morning Mom."

"Miles is out in the car with Mother waiting for the two of you. I placed some bagels and coffee in the limo for you. You'd better get going if you don't want to risk being on Mother's bad side. You know she doesn't like being late for church. Your father and I will join you there." She pushed us out the door and Miles was waving for us to join him in the car.

*Poor boy. I'd better go rescue him before my grandmother signs him up for a six-month concert series.*

"Sorry we're running a little late this morning." Lecia got in first and I followed behind her in search of the coffee and bagels that my mother had placed in containers in the back of the limo.

"Overslept again, vampire Cade?" My grandmother was aware of the nickname Lecia and Miles had given me, since my job required me to perform late nights and into the wee hours of the morning and catch up with sleep during the day.

"Honestly, I forgot Miles had the concert today." I took a bite of my bagel and ignored my grandmother's pursed lips and cutting eyes.

"Miles, listen to Grammie Mommy." She tapped him on the shoulder to get his attention. The car started up and we rolled down the driveway on our way to church.

"I know you can really get the crowd going with your fervor of the spirit, but can you move your head and shoulders more and your hips less? I'm not criticizing sweetheart, but we're a respectable Baptist church, and not the congregation of the rump shakers. I know my people and I don't want them to miss out on hearing your lyrics because they are distracted by your movements. You understand, don't you?"

"Yes, Grammie Mommy, but I can't always control the spirit."

"Well, there's spirit and there are things that are carnal. Put that word in your book—carnal—and we can study the differences and how to recognize the carnal things of the world."

Lecia looked out the window, distracted by her own thoughts instead of joining in the conversation.

"Lecia, do you want a bagel or a bite of mine?" I asked and took another sip of coffee.

"Oh, no thanks. I don't want to smear my lipstick." She turned her head and continued to gaze out of the window. *She's not going to help me, so I might as well take the solo plunge.*

"Grammie, don't you think a child who is nine years old is too young for a lesson on recognizing carnal things?"

"I started talking to you about those things at about the same age, and I'm proud to say that it's probably why you made such a fine choice of a wife and mother for your child because you knew about the carnal things."

*It never stopped me from finding and tasting the carnal pleasures of the world.*

"Thanks Grammie." She finally joined in and my grandmother continued her lecture with Miles.

"Alright, we're going to watch the hips; don't start the song with 'Let's do this,' and did you bring that tablet thing you like?"

He pulled the electronic tablet out of the car pocket and turned it on.

"Are you talking about this thing?"

"Yes, bring it in the sanctuary with you. It seems to stop you from fidgeting during the sermon. We're having the new associate pastor speak today and he's not as dynamic as Pastor Mike."

"Grammie, it's hard sitting there a long time."

"I know baby, and I give you credit for trying and agreeing to come with me to church anytime I ask. You're my good boy and I'm so proud of you."

"Thanks Grammy Mommie." Miles smiled at her.

I entered the sanctuary, followed by Lecia, Miles, and Grammie. I looked around and found a seat as fast as I could, as I had no intention of going to the front and risking falling asleep in front of everyone. Lecia sat beside me, and Miles was about to join us in our pew in the middle of the sanctuary, when an usher grabbed his hand and escorted him and Grammie to the front pew while a member of the choir came down and placed a tambourine in Miles's hand. My grandmother required a cane, and Miles was always sensitive to helping her in her seat and placing her cane beside her.

Act II: Playing with Fire

The children were called to the front of the assembly, and Miles was placed in front of the mic as the music started up. He swayed a little, then looked at his grandmother and restrained his movements while beating the tambourine. My chest swelled with pride as I knew he had a good singing voice, but I wasn't aware that he could work a crowd. By the end of the first verse, the crowd was on their feet, hands clapping and tapping their feet to the music while Miles kept time with the tambourine. He moved from side to side and down the aisle before the sensual hip movements started. I could only imagine if he was eighteen instead of nine years old, some would consider it a scandalous affair in the church. The song ended, and it took some time for the packed church to settle, as the spirit had indeed been awakened. My grandmother gave him a hug after he took his seat beside her, and she smiled like a puffed peacock in her elaborate hat and Sunday best suit.

The minister rose to begin his sermon at the pulpit and furrowed his brow after casting his attention on Miles, who was now playing with his tablet in the front row. The minister finished his prepared text, but it was his impromptu remarks that I feared raised my grandmother's dander. Ever since I was a little boy, I knew, and I had witnessed that the best way to incur Barbara Olivia Rogers's wrath was to talk about one of her children, especially in a public forum.

"Brothers and sisters, the spirit has gifted me to say this and I have to obey the spirit. Mother Barbara, you all are doing a fine job with that boy Miles. A mighty fine job indeed but—"

*Uh oh, I don't think he's aware he's walking in a loaded minefield.* I looked at Lecia and she was biting her lips as she looked up at the pastor.

"Too many of you parents are falling into the trap of letting your children play games and engage with social media, instead of admonishing them on the importance of listening to, the Word. Here's an example of what I'm saying. Miles, come forward and share what I talked about today."

I could only see the back of her head, but I knew my Barbaro. I shook my head and located my parents, sitting a few rows behind us before turning back to the front of the church to see my grandmother sitting erect with her shoulders tightly drawn to her side. Her image was captured on the big screens in front of the church, and she turned her head upwards as if deriving strength from heaven above. Miles got up from his seat and took his place in front of the congregation.

"Miles, can you tell the assembly what I spoke about today?"

"Yes sir. Your talk came from a lesson that we should not lose heart and tire from doing good. Your talk helped me to finish a poem I was working on for my Grammie Mommy Barbara Rogers, who is a hard worker in church and for our family."

My grandmother turned her attention to Miles and her eyes softened as she awaited his words.

"We study together, and I call this poem, 'A Tired Worker's Prayer.' I dedicate it to her because she helped me with some of the words.

In our toil and labors,
We perspire,
And we tire.
Despite that,
We're blessed,

Act II: Playing with Fire

If through it all,
We not let,
Our countenance fall.

Blessed,
If we discover,
Our hopes,
Our joys,
And our true desires.

There are no surrogates,
None others we can hire.
We must take the journey ourselves,
Even if while we tarry,
We grow tired.


We apply our crafts,
And produce objects,
Of great workmanship,
While we endure life's hardships.

Sometimes, we feel stuck in life's mire,
But we pray for great strength and fortitude,
And though through our toil,
We may tire,
We continue to walk bravely,
Through the fire.

Amen."


"Young man, you sure have a way with words." The
preacher clapped.

"Thank you. I love my family and I love words." Miles beamed a smile at Grammie Mommy.

"Well, Miles, I ask that your family members present today stand up with you, so we can acknowledge them. As I said, they are doing a great job with you."

We all rose in support of our son and grandson. I extended my hand to help Lecia to her feet, and my parents stood with us as the congregation applauded. Miles has the it factor; but I would have preferred if he wasn't put on the spot. I planned to go up to the front and gather him and my grandmother for a quick exit after we sat, and the benediction was said.

"Lecia, let's go get Miles and get out of here." I leaned over and whispered to her.

"Sure Cade, but I think he's alright. Many people are going up front to shake his hand."

"It's not Miles I'm worried about." We made our way up to the front of the church, but not before my grandmother and the minister were engaged in conversation.

"Pastor, do you see how packed the church was today?" my grandmother asked him.

"Yes, Mother Rogers we had a good crowd today."

"And have you noticed any time I ask Miles to come and sing for us the church is packed?"

"Well, I'd like to think the people don't come for a performance because they understand the importance of the Word."

"It's important to attract the young people with something that is relevant to them. I'm not sure what we gain in preaching to empty pews."

My mother made her way to the front and placed her hand gently on her mother's arms.

"Mother don't forget Cade and his family need to catch a plane tonight. We really need to be going."

"Lauren, you and everybody go to the car and I'll be there shortly. I have a little more to say and it shouldn't take long. Please do as I say."

"Alright Mother. We'll be waiting." I sighed, knowing if my mother couldn't convince Barbaro, I didn't stand a chance.

"Miles, go with your parents. I thank you for the poem and I hope you make a copy of it for me. You've always made your Grammie Mommy so proud." She turned her attention back to the minister and we departed down the aisle.

My grandmother kept her word, and it wasn't long before a deacon was walking alongside her to help her to the car.

"Thank you so much deacon."

"You're welcome Mother Rogers."

I hoped Miles wouldn't ask her, but he did.

"Grammie Mommy, what did you say to the minister?"

"Never you mind what I said, but I had a teachable moment with him and I think we'll both grow from it."

"Oh, I get it Grammie. It was grown people stuff." Miles lowered his head and resumed playing his game, and Grams tightened her lips and refused to say more about the incident.

# CHAPTER FOURTEEN

Miles had another performance for us to attend, but thankfully it was a concert on the grounds of the Institute for the patients and staff, and I didn't have to miss my own rehearsals at the club and recording sessions in downtown Washington to attend. We agreed that I would meet them at the auditorium, and I greeted Lecia with a kiss after I arrived and took my seat in the audience.

"Where's Miles? The show should be starting soon, and I didn't see him with the other kids. His teacher said she thought he was sitting with you in the audience and waiting for the show to begin. Unlike the other kids, she said he didn't need as much practice and wasn't prone to stage fright."

"No, he's not been with me. Let me check in the garden just outside the back door. He likes watching the butterflies and the bees."

"Alright, you go to the garden and I'll check the bathroom." I searched the nearest restroom and then the other one down the long corridor but still no signs of my son. I took the time to relieve myself and came out but was detained by another parent who wanted to introduce himself to me. I walked back inside the auditorium and Lecia had not returned to her seat. I looked around the auditorium and decided to go outside to the garden with hopes of finding them both there safe and enjoying a little sun before the performance. After exiting the back door, I ventured into the garden but stopped dead in my tracks, as I looked up and found Lecia seated in the shade on one of the stone benches with her back to me. Miles and his babysitter Brenda Hall were standing near another adult who sat in the sun wearing dark glasses and was smiling at Miles, who was flapping his arms like wings as he was undoubtedly sharing his current obsession: insects like butterflies, bees, and fireflies. I walked closer to join in the conversation and to remind them that the time to the start of the performance was drawing near.

"Miles," I called out, and Lecia turned to face me with sad eyes that glistened. Her skin was pale in the shade and her chin trembled slightly. I motioned to him by pressing my index finger to my watch. "Fifteen minutes to showtime buddy. A professional never leaves his audience waiting." I got to the bench and sat next to Lecia.

"Hi Pops. I won't be late. I was just explaining to my friend Jane how phenomenal bees are. Then Mami came and I introduced her to Mami and Brenda."

"Hi Mr. Moore. I'm glad I was able to beat the traffic and get here to support Miles. I'll take him backstage to his teacher and join you in our seats. Come on Miles. It's time to go."

"Break a leg Miles." Lecia rubbed her eyes and opened her arms for a hug from him before he left.

"Is everything alright Mami?"

"Yes Miles. I'm fine, you know my allergies bother me from time to time. You go ahead with Brenda and I'll be in the audience excited to hear that song you've been practicing. You sing like my little angel."

"Alright Mami but I'm not your little angel, I'm your big angel." He stretched his arms wide, flapping them in the air and stood on his toes. "See how big I am?"

"You have a big place in my heart Mijo. Now go with Brenda. I don't want your teacher and the other kids worried about where you are." He ran to the door and disappeared into the building, with Brenda following quickly behind him.

I took Lecia's hand and she looked up at the woman seated in front of her. She said nothing, but her grip tightened around my hand and I grimaced in pain and tried to wiggle my fingers to ensure my hand still had an adequate blood supply. The woman whose identity I already knew lowered her glasses and looked directly at Lecia with a smile on her face.

"Lecia, I'm so happy to see you after so many years. I prayed I would have an opportunity to speak to you again." She hesitated before continuing. "…To explain my actions."

Lecia's chest was heaving and her breath audible as she attempted to get up to depart, but I firmly held her hand, pulling her back to the bench.

"Miles has grown and he's such a charmer…. I'm nervous, Lecia, so I won't take much more of your time. I wanted you to know I've done well since my brain tumor was removed years ago, but I come back to the Institute for routine follow-ups because my tumor was considered rare and its effects on my behavior are currently being studied by researchers here. I want you to know I'm no longer a danger to you or Miles. He's such a joy." She pulled the shades from her eyes and placed her glasses in her lap. Her pupils constricted from the intensity of the sun, and she cupped her hand over her face. For the first time she looked at me.

"Cade, it's so good to see you again." Her smile was sickly, syrupy sweet, as she leaned her head to the side. Her pupils were dilated, and her eyes sparkled.

"Hello Darlene." My response was cool, and she turned her attention back to Lecia.

"Lecia, I hope one day we can be friends again."

"Darlene, that's not ever going to happen, and I would appreciate it if you would stay away from my son. I can't do this any longer." Her hand slipped out of mine and she departed. I got up to follow behind her and looked back at Darlene weakly waving her hand at me.

Lecia was in her seat next to Brenda by the time I made my way through the crowd, which I guessed yielded less to a tall grown man than a mother eager to get to her seat to support her child. In this arena, Miles and his mother were the rock stars. I sat next to her and took her hand in mine to await the opening of the heavy curtains. The staff member who knew sign language was on the stage performing after Miles insisted on an interpreter so that his best friend at the Institute, William Major, who had a brother who was deaf, could enjoy the performance as well as the other kids.

The show lasted about an hour and Miles was clearly the star. He sang, danced, and even convinced his teacher to let him use a few seconds of a rap verse he created for the song. I had to admit it, he was pretty good.

The performance ended; and I used the time to talk to Brenda while Lecia was backstage retrieving Miles.

"Brenda, thank you for coming to his performance and for staying with Miles tonight. He loves it when he knows others who care about him are in the audience cheering him on. His mother and I need some time to talk about the options his treatment team has presented to us."

"Not a problem Mr. Moore. I love spending time with Miles, and he's so disciplined for a kid his age. After he has dinner, a little mental break to play with his games and a snack, he's ready to spend time alone in his room playing music or writing things in one of his notebooks. He's very creative, and that gives me time to study my lesson. He has motivated me to be serious about my studies and to avoid distractions from my cell phone going off all the time." We turned to see Miles and Lecia coming back to join us.

"Miles you were fantastic." I hugged him and gave him a pat on the back.

"Thanks Pops, but I still can't hit some of the lower notes on some of my favorite songs."

"Miles, most kids can't hit those notes, and I have no doubt that you will someday soon. Your voice coach told me you can already move with little effort from one register to the other with consistent tone. Your skills are better than average, but let's not get caught up in vocal pedagogy right now. Brenda is going to take you home while I take care of some business with your mother."

"I'm still amazed at the conversations you have with Miles while my mother is stuck in battles with my younger brother about cleaning his room. Miles is one versatile kid. He gets along well with my parents, and my brother likes hanging out with him playing basketball and computer games."

Lecia broke into the conversation before I could convince her that we needed some private time.

"Cade, I wasn't prepared for an evening out. Can we postpone this until later?"

"No Lecia, we really need to address this today. Brenda and Miles will be fine. The limo driver is out front waiting for them and we can go in my car."

"Alright. Miles, you know the routine. Thank Brenda for helping out on such short notice."

"No problem Mrs. Moore. I hope you're able to mix a little pleasure with business tonight. Miles and I will be fine, and I know how to get in touch with the two of you. Come on Miles. We'd better get going if we want to beat the traffic on 495." She gathered their things and we all left the auditorium together. Lecia and I hadn't had a chance to talk about her encounter with Darlene, and I didn't want to put it off. We got into the car and I knew my wife doesn't do well with an immediate onslaught of questions, so I decided it was best to follow her lead and wait until she began the conversation. I hadn't anticipated the painfully silent drive in traffic to the restaurant in downtown Washington at the Mayflower Hotel, where I had a private table reserved for us at Edgar's.

Our wine was on the table when we arrived, and the waiter had just delivered our meals when she asked her first question.

"How long have you known she was getting care at the Institute? The very same place our son has been receiving care for the past year?" I took my first of many sips of wine tonight and I hoped she would start sipping on hers.

"Ahh, this wine is superb." I swirled another mouthful in my mouth and swallowed before I answered. "I've known she was there the entire time."

She closed her eyes tight and opened them but took a mouthful of wine from her glass before she responded.

"My, my. This wine is very good."

*I hope good enough to make this discussion as painless as possible.*

"You always have a reason for the things you do, so tell me the reason why you would keep something like this from me?"

"Every time I tried to mention her name to you, I ran into the same wall. You'd tear up and say—"

"Please keep that damn woman's name out of your mouth or there's nothing you can say about her that I need to hear." She finished my sentence.

"I'm glad you remembered that, Lecia, and maybe we can get through this discussion without blaming each other. I didn't know how to get past the wall you had thrown up when it came to her. I had to bear that burden of knowing she was at the Institute without you, but I made sure our son stayed safe. He has benefitted so much from understanding his condition and learning to control his temper with treatment at the Institute. Dar—"

"You can say her name and its time I hear the whole story."

"She has been very cooperative, and she's always been under surveillance. I don't know if you saw the ankle bracelet she was wearing, which was one of the terms of her treatment versus facing charges and probable incarceration. Remember, you didn't want her prosecuted and you were right. There was a reason for her behavior."

"She really had a brain tumor?"

"Yes, she had a brain tumor, which has been removed. She's calmer and the hostility that surfaced every time your name was mentioned is gone. She speaks more with regret and missing your friendship." We both finished our glasses of wine.

"I forgave her and I'm glad she's better, but I could never be her friend again. The issue of continuing Miles's treatment at the Institute after the end of this month is a no-brainer for me. I just don't know where to transfer his care at this point."

"Lecia, are you sure about it? Let's take our time deciding on our next move. Our son has moved a lot in his short life, and he's made good friends here. I don't know if we should move him further away from the family at this point."

"Cade, she still loves you and I saw it in her eyes. It's not completely over for her."

"And it never had a beginning for me. She was a fan gone rogue. I've worked through my anger toward her and my feelings are about as good as I could hope for, regarding Darlene. She's a neutral for me and I don't loathe her like I used to. I am more concerned about you right now. Tell me how you're feeling. I know Darlene is a trigger for many emotions for you."

I took in a bite of my meal and waited for her to respond to me.

"You're right, she's a trigger for me—a trigger for many emotions, but mostly anger. My relationship with her was just another example of why the it's-just-you-and-me relationships don't last."

"What do you mean? I think we've got a good track record for a you-and-me relationship. We've been together since the first night we spent together."

"I know that Cade, but my past sometimes is a barrier, although not often in our relationship. I came into this world with a special you-and-me relationship with my twin brother, and it was over after three years. I met Darlene and at first she was the best friend a girl could have—another you-and-me relationship—and look at us now."

"I see." I put down my fork and grabbed her hands. "Are you worried if the relationship we share will last?"

"I don't obsess about it Cade, but I would be lying if situations like some of our friends divorcing doesn't make those thoughts cross my mind."

"Those thoughts never cross my mind Lecia. I didn't lose a twin and I don't know the pain of that, but I know you're my soul's twin, my ying to your yang or my yang to your ying. I'm not sure which one, but I have no doubt that you're the missing part of me that my soul set out on its quest to find and I'm happy I found you."

"Thanks Cade, but I worry more about Miles placing any person who tried to come between us on his list." We both laughed, more from being nervous than amused. We both knew Miles, still kept a list, although he thought he was being discrete about it.

"Speaking of Miles. He's the best example of you-and-me in the world."

"You're right Cade. He's been a gift of our love."

"And, there's Cadejazz Entertainment in addition to the success of the group Fortune."

"Why are you giving me credit? It's your talent and business skills that have made your ventures a success."

"Thanks, but I couldn't have done it without your love and support. You stood by me when I was a struggling artist and you believed in me. I don't worry about coming home to a jealous tirade, and you've made our home a peaceful retreat for us." She loosened her hands from mine.

"I think I'm getting my appetite back and the food does look good." She picked up her fork and took a few bites before dabbing the corners of her mouth with her napkin.

"Having Miles has given me the credentials I needed in my practice too. The walls in my office were covered with degrees and awards, but there were always some mothers who respectfully listened to my advice and invariably asked the question, are you a mother Dr. Tavares? When I answered no, there was the nod of the head and maybe a twist of the lips. Some mothers even told me, 'Until you're a mother, you couldn't understand.' I had Miles and I haven't heard those comments on any occasion since I've done part-time contract work at the clinics in Maryland."

"Are you willing to give up your contract work Lecia? We've all made contacts and friendships since we relocated here. We have a way of life that for now is working for us, and we can commute between here and New York or here and North Carolina without much difficulty."

"I'm not sure if I want to raise Miles mainly in New York, and after the incident with Austin's friend, Joshua Holmes, and your family's response to it, I'm concerned about their overindulgence of Miles. I saw what overindulgence did to Mario, and I don't want to risk the same thing happening to Miles."

"I have to agree with you and I also have concerns. When it comes to the two youngest grandchildren in the family, Miles and Aria, their shit never stinks." I laughed.

"Graphic, but that's still putting it mildly. Miles and Aria, I meant NeNe, are developing a very enmeshed relationship with each other and a little distance I think will be good for the two of them in the long run. Miles is forming additional relationships with children his age, and Dana said that other than the relationship with her sister, NeNe doesn't have a female playmate."

"She's still young Lecia." I hoped she would let it go but she didn't.

"She's eleven years old Cade, and other than family members, NeNe doesn't spend a lot of time with girls, but I think we should continue to focus on our issues."

"Lecia, I thought I should ask you again about joining me on a quick gig in Stockholm." She began shaking her head and resumed eating.

"Listen to me first. I owe a friend a favor who's starting a new venture in Smooth Jazz Cruising, and he asked me to join them when they reach the port of Stockholm. We can board the ship there, and I'll perform that night with the house band and Pete. Then we'll have two days to relax aboard ship and disembark in Copenhagen."

"Cade, I don't want to be cooped up with Miles in a small suite for three days while you're working. He's older now and I don't want to think about his resistance to being dragged along with us."

"I've thought about that Lecia, and the suite is not small but spacious and luxurious with a balcony for viewing sunrises and sunsets over the water and there's plenty of space for us. Miles will have his own room, and there will be a room for Angelique, who agreed to come with us on the cruise to spend time with Miles at night. There are also great 'tween and teen programs aboard the ship."

"So Cade, you're not above bribing our child?"

"I don't consider it a bribe, and I think we all need a break from everything that has happened in the past year."

"I do agree with that."

"Can I consider the matter settled then?"

"Sure, why not? It does sound like fun." Lecia took another bite of her food.

"Good, what do you want for dessert—and don't say pie?" I joked.

She looked up at me and laughed. It was nice to hear her carefree giggle again.

# CHAPTER FIFTEEN

We were enjoying a pleasant sunny day at sea on the pool deck of the cruise ship, seated in lounge chairs in our bathing suits when Miles came to join us with his plate of food containing a hamburger, hotdog, chips, and cookies. Lecia had loosened his dietary restrictions and allowed him to have food with empty calories and a little, more sweets.

"We're on vacation and I'm not about to waste the time being the food police." She looked at Miles, who was smiling brightly. The decision to loosen the reigns on him was a strategic save, since when he was relaxed, it was easier for us to enjoy time together as a family. Bringing Angelique was working out just fine. She was often busy dancing and chatting with a young cruiser during the day while giving us the freedom to party with the other adults at night.

"Mami and Pops, this is the best." He sat in a chair next to ours.

"Are you having a good time buddy?"

"I am, and the food is great. I just found out I won the amateur talent contest today. Pops, can I perform with you tonight? I'm good at playing the guitar and I can take Medhi's place."

"Miles, you know I have an adult show and I have a house musician for my performance tonight. Mr. Pete is here to help me too, but I appreciate your offer. Maybe when we get back home, I can include a performance by you on one of the songs on my next album. Matter of fact, I've been working on a new song and there's a piece in the hook that may be ideal for you."

"Alright." He took the first bite of his hamburger and closed his eyes in delight while tapping his feet and bobbing his head to the beat of a popular song playing over the speakers.

*Nothing like music and food to calm the passions of my fire producing son.*

Lecia lowered the frames of her glasses and looked at Angelique shaking it and tossing her head as she danced to the music.

"So Miles, no feelings about Angelique and the time she's been spending with her new suitor? She's had to divide her time between babysitting you and spending time with him."

"What kind of feelings? Are you talking about me being jealous? Eww, Angelique was my babysitter when I was a kid and she's my companion now."

"Yes Lecia, Miles and I agreed that he could use a companion and not a babysitter."

"Pardon me, I wasn't a part of those negotiations."

"Mami, Angelique is cool and she's pretty, but she's too old for me. It's her that needs a babysitter and not me. I had to tell some other guys who upset her by brushing against her to stop since she was my companion not theirs. Her friend is nice, and she smiles a lot when he's around, unlike the other guy who was talking to her yesterday."

"Well Miles, I don't want you to spend your time thinking you have to protect Angelique."

"Don't worry Mami. She took me to the gym and we sparred with each other. She put me in a headlock and tossed me to the mat. She's teaching me self-defense skills."

"We were up early this morning and I saw some of the moves she was demonstrating for him. They were more self-defensive and not aggressive moves for fighting." I knew

Lecia needed the reassurance that Miles wasn't receiving more tools as weapons. He already had many of them.

He wolfed down his food and stretched out on his lounger with his shades drawn over his eyes.

"Pops, I'm going to be a musician like you and go all over the world playing music and eat anything I want."

"Sounds like fun, and it can be great being a musician, but remember that it's hard work and it requires commitment. Your fans deserve your best, and they'll return it a thousand fold in applause and gratitude. I thought you were interested in being an engineer or an architect like your uncle?"

"That was before I knew how happy I was making music like you."

"You have a lot of time to decide what you want to do with your life," I told him and closed my eyes to focus on the feeling of the sun warming my body. I was about to drop off to sleep when I thought I heard Lecia asking Miles about Darlene.

"So Miles, what did you share with Jane?"

"Not much Mami. She knows my name of course and I told her how old I was. She kept telling me I reminded her of someone before I told her you were my mom and I told her Pops name. She said she loved how I danced and made everyone happy. She said something about my looks and I told her I was my mother's son and I looked like you."

"You did?" I kept my eyes shut and my ears tuned to the conversation.

"Abuela has always told me I get my good looks from you and I have a big heart like you. She said Pops was a very good musician, but he needed to practice his dancing."

"Well, we can't be great at everything."

"Mami, I don't think you really like Jane."

"I don't know your friend Jane and I can't say I trust her."

"She's not my friend Mami. She's a sad lady that I wanted to make smile, that's all."

"Miles, come join me on the dance floor!" Angelique yelled and waved to him as she waited for him to join in with the other dancers.

"Coming Angelique."

"Go Miles and have some fun. You're a great dancer." Lecia smiled and encouraged him.

"Thanks Mami and so are you."

She settled back in the chair and placed her glasses back on.

"You can stop pretending Cade. I'm aware that every closed eye isn't asleep."

"You're quoting my grandmother way too much Lecia. Get some rest because the show will probably last into the wee hours of the morning and I plan to have some adult fun while we're here. This is a working vacation." She raised herself on her elbows and looked around the deck.

"Why are there so many women wearing skirts with upside-down pineapple prints on them or guys with shirts embellished with pineapples?"

"They are swingers, baby, and don't ever ask me to buy you one."

"To each his own Cade, but satisfying your appetite is a lot for this girl." She settled back in her chair and fell asleep.

"Hey cruisers, let's do this." I picked up my horn to the applause of the audience and began playing one of Lecia's favorite songs and a big seller for the band, a smooth jazz composition I entitled, "I'll Always Belong to You."

"I don't want to sit in the front Cade. I'll take a seat at the bar." She hadn't attended many of my shows since Miles came along, and it was probably to my advantage that she got a wider view of the audience by sitting off to the side of the room. It was a routine performance of fifteen songs, and the usual things occurred. Bits of paper and business cards were thrown along the side of the stage for the roadies to collect. Women reached out their hands for me to touch, and the more extroverted members of the audience were sensual in their dancing and effusive in their declarations of love for me. *All in a day's work.*

I intentionally came off the stage knowing well that I faced being groped by some of my more enthusiastic fans, who were already in an alcohol-infused frenzy. My virtue was spared as I wasn't groped, but I had a pocketful of cards and requests to come to multiple cabins before we made it back to port.

I gave Pete a chance to display his solo skills in several songs before returning and ending the set. I returned backstage and allowed the fans to file out before joining Lecia and my friend, Daniel Palmer, the musical director for the cruise at the bar. I needed to talk to him in front of Lecia about the arrangements we'd made regarding my appearance on the cruise. We were seated alone in the room except for the bartender, who excused himself to restock the bar.

"Is my love suite available and have you kept the location of it a secret from the staff? Remember, you agreed that it would be on a different floor from our family suite?" I reminded him.

"Cade, it's ready and the only reason I agreed to it is because you told me you would discuss it with me in front of Lecia. I didn't want any trouble if she found out about it. You all aren't swingers, are you?" Lecia sputtered on her drink and grabbed a napkin to clean the liquid off the bar.

"No we're not Dan." She struggled to get out the words.

"Cade what is this about? Is a love suite part of your rider now?" She waited for my answer and I reached out to touch her before explaining my actions. She always did better when I closed the distance between us while we were discussing issues that could go sour if I wasn't careful.

"I'm not aware of an additional suite being a part of an industrywide rider, but some entertainers always maintain their own sex pad. I just wanted to share some time with you alone doing some adult things."

"I don't understand why you have to call it that." She lowered her head and covered her eyes just before the bartender came back to refresh our drinks. "What, a sex pad? You will baby."

"I'm going to leave the two of you alone to discuss things, but please, Lecia, don't tell my wife I went along with this little surprise. There's no way I'm going to convince her that you were in on whatever plans Cade has for tonight since it will only ignite a firestorm of suspicions that I have a fuck pad too."

"Sure Dan. I won't let you get caught up in my husband's devious plans." I gave her a sideways glance and waved goodbye to Dan after he gulped down his drink and left the room. I looked at Lecia after savoring my Scotch and licked my lips.

"It's going to be good baby. You'll see. I've let Angelique know how to contact us if an emergency arises. Are you ready to go?"

"You're twisted Cade." She accepted my kiss on her lips.

"But you still love me." Our relationship was based on a foundation of love and trust. I knew she'd get that I just wanted us to enjoy each other and not waste time worrying about my infidelity. That wasn't me and she knew it.

I placed my glass on the bar and took her hand to lead her to the suite.

I opened the door to room 919 at the end of the hall and the lights had been dimmed in the room, which was filled with an assortment of roses, tulips, and greenery arranged in crystal vases. A bottle of her favorite wine was chilling in a crystal ice bucket by the bedside with a note tied to the neck of the bottle: "Do not open and start the fun without me. Wait babe until I get here."

I led Lecia into the room and closed the door behind us to have privacy while I nipped on her neck and cupped her ass, pressed against the door. I attempted to lead her to the bed, with red rose petals spread on top of a white Egyptian linen duvet, but she hesitated in joining me on the bed, where I'd planned a night of lovemaking.

"Wait a minute Cade. I'll be right back. I need to use the bathroom."

She turned around, opened the door to the small space, and began gritting her teeth while I sat back on the bed, observing her abrupt change in behavior.

"Get. Out of. My. Room." She spoke through her tightened lips and looked at me with narrowed eyes just as a naked woman spilled out of the bathroom and onto the floor. I jumped back in surprise as a woman I hadn't seen before crawled away from Lecia and in my direction, with Lecia moving quickly behind and about to dive on her. I leaped off the bed across the naked interloper and grabbed Lecia before things got nasty. Her chest was heaving, and I placed my arms around her cautiously but firmly and turned her away from the woman before throwing her the robe hanging on a peg in front of me for cover. Lecia took deep breaths and looked back at her after calming a bit.

"Why are you here?" Her skin was warm to touch and the wild look in her eyes had returned.

"Cade, did you have anything to do with this hussy coming here tonight?"

"No Lecia." *Well not directly but my coming and going in and out of the room multiple times earlier today probably resulted in clues where my room was located. I hope she paid the cabin stewards handsomely for their assistance.*

The woman just stood there looking at us and was about to say something, but I held my hand up to warn her to hold her peace until after I got a firmer grip on Lecia's arms.

"My wife asked you to leave, and I think you should and never come back. We'll act like this didn't happen and not report you to security if you don't come close to me or my family again. I don't want this to be any more embarrassing than it already is." She scrambled to her feet and drew the robe around her before scurrying out the door. I held Lecia in silence and eased her to the bathroom.

"You were about to use the bathroom, weren't you? Calm down and I'll be right here at the door waiting for you when you're ready to come out. Take all the time you need and just remember I love you." I kissed the few tears that had escaped and fallen down her cheeks.

She went into the bathroom and relieved herself while I ran and poured two glasses of wine but was delayed by having to refill my glass after taking a few gulps. The wine was chilled to perfection and I ran back to the door with two glasses in hand and gave her a glass as she exited the bathroom. I held her as she leaned against my chest and she took a small sip of wine.

"Let's sit on the couch." She nodded and went without hesitation. She looked at the bed and turned her back to it while she sipped the wine and fell against my chest with my arms around her, stroking her shoulders.

"Are you trying to demonstrate to me that you could have your choice of women tonight?" She sat up and extended her hand.

"I had nothing to do with that woman being here Lecia."

"Well, that only answers one of my questions. Hmm, let's see your other choices. Empty your pockets Cade."

I placed my drink on the table in front of us and emptied my pockets of business cards and bits of paper. She placed her drink on the table and began looking through the messages.

"Let me turn you on lover boy…. I'll make you forget all your problems…. Let me rock your world; how original your fans are." She grabbed the papers in a ball and hurled it at the trash can before looking up at me with an icy stare.

"Do you know I could be kicking that woman's tail right now and scratching your eyes out for good measure? Is this what it's like for you every night on the road? Some woman trying to get in your room?"

I took a chance with my response, but I was hoping we could move past this moment without the threat of violence.

"It could be that way if I wanted it to be, but I'm faithful to you and content to come home to my family or Facetime with you and Miles in my absence. It's calming for me to talk to you after I leave the stage." She picked up her glass and rubbed the rim against her lips before looking at me again.

"You do call every night when you're away or come home when time and expenses allow you to."

"Lecia, infidelity can be the hollow experience of any man in the public eye. I have had women throwing themselves at me before I had my first hit record. I'm not a bad-looking fellow. Women do want me." I nuzzled her neck and she drew back away from me.

*Oops, too soon, my bad.*

"I never said you were bad looking Cade, or unattractive. You're my man and I know you're talented and generous. I also know I've hit the lottery in winning your love, and I've not been jealous before because you've never given me a reason to be before tonight." She grabbed her shoulders and, holding herself, began rocking back and forth. I placed my hand on her shoulder to stop her movement and turned her chin to face me.

"Lecia, if you knew that there was always the remote possibility of me being with another woman, and there were many women before I met you, why have you held on to this fantasied belief that you, me, and Darlene were somehow involved in a sick love triangle or feel that it matters that she may still have feelings for me?"

"I don't know Cade. I just never looked at it like that before."

"Darlene was one of tens of women who frequented the club before I met you. I slept with some of them but not with Darlene. You remember what Miles said about her earlier today? His description couldn't have been more accurate."

"Yes I do. He said she was a sad woman whom he didn't mind sharing his talent with to make her smile." I nodded and placed my hand on her cheek.

"I could see Darlene was looking for love and I was never going to be the one who gave it to her. Miles saw her loneliness and so did I. You've been the only one who couldn't see the real picture of your former friend."

"Maybe because sadness was something we shared. I was sad too at my core after I lost my twin brother and my parents never wanted to talk about him, but that didn't stop you from falling in love with me while Darlene worshipped you."

"She worshipped the public persona she thought she knew, and unlike her, your sadness never made you bitter or lose your capacity to rejoice in the happiness and success of others. That's what I saw in you Lecia. A woman with a sad but big heart who loved people. I wanted you and needed you to love me."

She let me draw nearer and I pulled her into my arms and rested my chin on top of her head while I rubbed her arms and placed kisses on her cheeks.

"So tell me, why me Cade? Why did you fall in love with me?"

"Do we still have to address the reason why I fell in love with you at this point in our marriage? Why does any man fall in love with a woman? Do you want me to say something logical about falling in love?"

"I know it's not easily explained, but it's important for me to know your thoughts if we're to put this behind us. I need you to try to tell me why. Please Cade. You've given me your name, you've given me generous gifts, the most special gift being our son, and you've tried to show me with your cock but never with words?"

"Oh, Lecia, I so love it when you let my cock do the talking. Can I use that language of my love while I gather my thoughts?" I kissed her deeply, filling her mouth with my hungry tongue before nibbling my way down to her collarbone. I loosened the buttons on her blouse and revealed her black laced bra.

"Te amo Mami. Are those words not enough?" I moved her bra to the side and began sucking her breast with just the right amount of pressure needed to make her nipples pucker.

"Me haces sentir muy bien Papi. It feels so good." She arched her back and helped me get rid of her blouse while I loosened her bra as fast as I could unhook the thing. Normally I had nimble fingers, but I fumbled with the hooks and she laughed while placing her hands behind her back and unhooked the damn thing with ease.

"There, now was that so hard?" She flung her bra on the floor.

"If you think you're going to get me out of this skirt without talking to me, think again, mi amor."

"Lecia, stop taunting me. Can't you see you've got me horny as hell." I pointed to my groin.

"Well let me get up so you can cool off." She got off the couch before I could grab her and went to get the remote. She bent over, showing me her ample ass, and looked at the tv to search for channels.

"They taped your performance, didn't they? And we can view it on demand, can't we? I want to see you perform the song, 'I'll Always Belong to You,' again. Maybe that will inspire you to come up with something."

I turned my head to the side to get a view of her black panties peeking from under her skirt, which was hiked up around her buttocks as she leaned over showing me her thighs and exciting every nerve in my body. I looked at the performance for a few seconds before crawling on the bed.

"Come join me Lecia. I'm tired and looking at me working isn't making me feel energetic."

"I'll turn the screen away, but I want to listen to the music. I love that song Cade."

"Alright but come to bed and I'll talk." I reached out my hand and guided her to the pillow, where I spread her hair out and looked down at my beautiful angel.

"Do I tell you often enough how gorgeous you are and how I can see your beauty even in the eyes of men who covet you?"

"I could always hear it again." She batted her eyes.

"Well, you are beautiful, inside and out. Maybe that's why I like looking at men looking at you. It always magnifies what I see when I look at you. It tells me that it's not some delusion that you're mine and other men would kill to have you." I loosened the button on her skirt and pulled at the zipper, as my erection got harder listening to the sound of the zipper, slowly descend down her back.

"Lift your hips so I can get you out of this. It's hindering my movements. No, I meant my thoughts." She lifted her hips and I helped her out of the skirt.

"More wine, baby?"

"No I want to be alert and focused on every word you say."

"Well, in order for me to be focused only on you, I'll need to be inside you." I rolled on top of her, kissed her breasts, and rolled my hips against her pelvis before settling down deep in her heat, filling her with my dick, hot and throbbing. My eyes rolled in the back of my head and my jaw dropped in ecstasy.

"Don't move Lecia. Oh, you feel so good. If you move, I'll lose my train of thought."

She lay quietly beneath me but began to move slowly and deliberately against me, in small circular motions, as I sunk deeper inside despite my desire that she not move.

"Talk to me Cade." My thoughts were short-circuiting with lust, but I managed to string some words together.

"That's it Lecia."

"What's it, baby?" She grabbed my biceps tightly and opened her legs, giving me greater access to that special spot inside her I hoped to find.

"I'm just Cade—with you. My soul can be exposed, and I feel safe with you. I'm my authentic self with you, warts and all."

"What else baby? Your words are music to my ears." She continued the slow grind and gyrated her hips, causing me to involuntarily grimace, as I looked down at her face glistening with sweat and her pupils dilating with pleasure. The song continued in the background and the scent of our lust and lovemaking filled the air.

"You're the key that has opened up everything locked inside of me. You're the reason I release music I didn't know I had inside me." I grabbed her and turned our bodies to place her on top and to slow down my climax, which was edging me toward a volcanic eruption. She tilted her pelvis upward as I pulled back from deep inside of her to share more of my thoughts as I thrusted, nice and slow.

"You've carried my son inside of you and in my mind, you'll always be blood of my blood, bone of my bones and flesh of my flesh. You're my lover, my best friend, my wife and I'm so lucky to have you in my life. You'll forever be a part of me Lecia." She arched her back and began moving up and down on me with a disinhibition that was uncommon for her. She started moaning louder, and I was thrusting like a man possessed, my balls slapping against her firm ass. Tension was mounting, and within seconds, we were both over the edge. I turned her again, grabbing her hips to let her take in every drop of me and I kissed her repeatedly, brushing my lips against hers as we recovered our breathing together.

"Thank you, baby. I could've died in this moment and felt life owed me nothing. You make me feel so good Lecia."

"That was beyond great Cade." I knew she was stroking my male ego and I loved it.

I took her into my arms, covering her with a full embrace of arms and legs flung around her to show how precious she was to me. I would always protect her with my body and my strength.

"I love you Lecia."

"I love you Cade and thank you for sharing your thoughts with me."

We lay in each other's arms for a few minutes listening to a few more songs before I took the remote and turned off the television.

"Lecia, I knew you were from North Carolina the night I met you in New York, and that was like an instant connection between us. I had seen you before on television, supporting a charity when I went home to Charlotte, prior to the night you came to see me at the club.

 "And I knew of your family's standing in the community, but it wasn't like we ran in the same social circles." She added while caressing my cheek.

"True, and despite that, I was Cade. Plain ol' Cade and not some successful businessman's son. With you, I had my own personal aura and I didn't have to worry about the bright sun of the accomplished Moore family shining on me. It didn't matter to you that I was Vincent and Doris Moore's younger brother. I could grow in my own light and I saw us growing together as we both sought out our own true destiny. I could reach for the skies with you and not worry about falling back to earth a failure. You helped me to see that what

I was aspiring to do with my life was worth it and not another pipe dream. I found myself, Lecia, in your belief in me, and I hope I gave that gift back to you." She stroked my chest and lifted her head to kiss me.

"You did Cade and you've given so much more. I needed your help to deal with my thoughts about Darlene and with those lingering insecurities; now I can put them to rest. I love you Cade for all those reasons. I have my you-and-me relationship again and you've helped me to feel whole and not fragmented by grief. For me, it's always been only you."

"Thank you, babe, for sharing with me, and it might be a little late to ask you, but I haven't seen you take your pill since we got onboard. Did you take it today?"

"No Cade, and I haven't taken the pill in almost a year."

"You didn't tell me you changed your birth control."

"I didn't change it because I don't need it. We haven't gotten pregnant in nine years despite trying for a year when Miles was five years old."

"So you're not worried about it?"

"Nope. Not at all Cade. Let's get under the covers." She settled back in my arms as I wrapped her in the duvet. "I'm tired and the wine is starting to get to me. I've enjoyed sharing your fringe benefits tonight."

"No, thank you babe. I think it's important to spice it up sometimes even if things didn't go as I had planned." My phone on the nightstand started buzzing and the caller ID lit up, displaying my manager's number. I hit end call, promising to call Ian back later in the morning. Lecia had fallen off to sleep and was breathing quietly in my arms.

I awoke from sleep minutes later with the phone buzzing in my ear again. Lecia had turned away from me and remained asleep despite the noise from the phone piercing the silence of the room. I gently pulled back the covers and hopped out of bed with the phone pasted to my ear, on the way to the bathroom for a multi-purpose stop.

"What the hell Ian? This had better be good. You got me out of bed and interrupted my sleep with my wife." I turned on the lights and looked at the angry mug staring back at me in the mirror before placing the phone on speaker to relieve myself.

"Really dude? You're taking a leak while talking to me?"

"What do you want?" Ian Caswell had been my manager for over ten years and we had a love-hate relationship, but mostly one of respect.

"Cadester, I got two offers for the band and we have to move on one or the other soon. I have a great deal for the band to return to Europe; your fans really miss you. Or we have a smoking deal to play the west coast, with multiple dates for you to play for your fan base, which has grown tremendously since the release of the last album. You're hot Cadester."

"Don't call me Cadester. It's too early for that shit."

"I've a flight booked for you and the family for later today to head out to California to discuss the deal with the promoters and backers in person. I want to make sure it's a good fit before you decide one way or the other. A mistake at this point in your career could cost us tens of millions. Connect with you later today. Bye."

"Ian!" *So much for the long weekend of relaxation. Lecia and Miles will understand.*

"I need some sleep. I'm going back to bed." I was talking to myself as I trudged back to my spot under the covers and fell back asleep.

# CHAPTER SIXTEEN

I didn't sleep as well as I had hoped and kept my shades on, as I slumped into one of the oversized club chairs on the plane.

"Cade, I've changed my mind about us needing to leave Maryland as soon as possible, especially since you placed things in a different context for me last night. Do we really need to upend our lives by relocating so quickly?" She placed her hand on top of mine, rubbing my skin slowly before inserting her index finger in the web space between my thumb and index finger. Like reflex, I encircled her finger as she thrusted it back and forth between the space. I opened my eyes and smiled. Miles was in the corner engrossed in writing in his new composition book.

"Lecia, I know it will be a sacrifice, but it could be a golden opportunity for all of us. One of the tour backers is also on the board of a hospital, and they've seen your resume. He's certain he could get you an appointment on staff, and now that Miles is older, he won't need you at home as much."

"He has made great friends Cade. I don't want to take him away from William, Rashad, and Greg." Miles looked at Lecia and placed his journal in his lap.

"Mami, I'll miss my friends, especially William, but I made other friends on the ship who live in California. Remember, you met Parker Middleton and his mom. Parker said if I come to California, he could be my manager; and the other boys who were in the talent show with me, have a garage band and they said I could be a part of the group, if you let us practice at our new house. Please Mami and Pops, say we can move to California. I like singing and dancing and I want to be a part of a band or maybe someday go out on my own."

The plane ran into a little turbulence and we all shook in our seats as we continued on our way to Los Angeles.

"More turbulence is ahead. Please buckle your seat belts." The captain's voice came over the loudspeaker and we obliged his directions. The beverage service was suspended as we raced through the clouded skies on our way to the west coast. I was looking forward to some refreshments, but who could complain when traveling aboard a luxury Lear jet. I took off my shades and placed them in my shirt pocket.

"You're only nine years old Miles. I don't think you need a manager at this point, and what about the plans for college? I thought you wanted to explore other interests than music."

"I could do it all Pops. You and Mami have always told me I have many gifts. I can find people to invest in my talent just like you're doing."

My phone rang, and it was Ian again. I answered and placed it on speaker.

"Cade, there's a slight change of plans. The primary backer has a sick kid and won't be able to meet with you in LA. He lives about sixty miles away in Palmdale and has an office and conference room there that's large enough for all interested parties to attend. I'll have a car waiting to take you to the meeting as soon as you land. Am I on speakerphone?"

"Yes Ian." He knew I often used speakerphone.

"Pardon my manners. Hi Lecia."

"Hi Ian."

"Cade, I know you wanted to take Lecia house hunting with a realtor, and I have a great team available to escort her around the city, if the two of you are comfortable with that. Lecia, do you mind looking at homes by yourself?"

"I was looking forward to looking at homes together," Lecia answered.

"I don't know about that one Ian." I shook my head and spoke up. "Especially since we haven't decided to relocate to California and I told you we were bringing Miles with us."

"Hey buddy. How are you doing Miles?"

"I'm fine Uncle Ian." He picked up his journal and began writing in it again.

"I remembered, and I have a wonderful surprise for Miles. I was able to arrange the desert tour you wanted for the two of you, about thirty-five miles away from Palmdale; and an added bonus is, they're filming an action film out there and a friend who owed me a favor, scored me two or three tickets if you all wanted an up-close viewing of the action scene in which they blow up a few buildings."

"With explosives and everything?" Miles bounced in his seat.

"That's what they told me," Ian responded, roping Miles into the plans to move to California.

"Cool. Pops, say we can go."

"I can't be in so many places at one time Ian." I sat up in my seat and frowned.

"Super hombre, listen, I've got you covered. I have two guys on the security team we use out here who are free to escort Miles until you get out of the meeting. The driver will take you to the filming as soon as the meeting is over and wait for the two of you to meet Lecia for dinner, if she wants to stay in LA and take her time looking at properties. You know our homes belong to our wives and she has great taste.

If she likes the home, chances are you'll like the home too. A happy wife is a happy life." I looked at Lecia and she shrugged her shoulders.

"Ian, I'll get back to you before we land with our plans."

"Alright, discuss it among yourselves and get back to me soon. Miles met Todd and Bernie, top-notch security guys when you toured in Europe. They've been transferred to the California detail."

"I remember them Uncle Ian. They're fun."

"Yes, they told me you were great when they were assigned to you. So, get back to me Cade. Bye."

"Bye Ian." "Bye Uncle Ian," we said in unison and I ended the call.

"What do you think about those plans Lecia?"

"I thought we could house hunt together but I'm alright looking without you, at this point. We can videotape the tour like we did when we moved to Maryland; and go back if we decide to move to California, and I was impressed with Todd and Bernie," she responded, and Miles nodded.

"I don't think Miles wants to spend the day looking at homes with me."

"Mami, as long as I have a bedroom with the sun coming in my room and I have a room to practice with my band, I won't complain. You pick great homes for us."

"Alright, we'll divide and conquer today. I agree with Miles that you're great at picking out a home, but I have a few requests. No morning sun in our bedroom, a home study, and a home studio that I can renovate if necessary, to my specifications."

"Got it Cade, so call Ian and finalize the plans with him. We're all going to have one busy day."

Act II: Playing with Fire

I liked the plans for a tour of the west coast, with many concerts that would earn me a hefty profit, while allowing me to stay close enough to LA and to Lecia and Miles. The European tour, on the other hand, required longer time away from the family and I had to play venues I had seen many times before. I reflected on my options, as I sat in the back of the limo after completing the initial negotiations with potential investors for the tour. *Enough about the future.* Today, I planned to spend time with Miles and then meet up with Lecia for dinner.

The dry desert scenery was lit with bright sun, and dark lava rocks were scattered around the ground and in the mountain crevices. A few Joshua trees were located close to the set, providing little precious shade, and mountains of beige sand stretched before us as far as I could see.

We arrived at the filming site and I got out of the car, leaning away from the oppressive heat assaulting my face. I put on my shades before heading to the largest trailer on the movie set, labeled visual effects crew. Bernie told me they would wait there for me before going to the observation point to safely view the explosions. I looked around at the movie set, which simulated a lone street leading to a brick veneered, prefab factory building that was made of plaster and appeared to be in the middle of nowhere. I read the script on the drive over, and the scene they were filming was about a spy ring who had a central building as their place of operations, at a secret isolated location. The most talented hackers from around the world, had been gathered for cyberwarfare, by a sinister mastermind bent on controlling international intelligence and selling the information to the highest bidder, on the dark web. The mastermind had an archenemy who had discovered the location, after he penetrated his nemesis's empire with his own spies and was going to destroy the building, and all the hackers who had not agreed to work with him.

"Hi Todd. I hope I'm not too late to see the action. The meeting went on longer than I planned. Where's Miles and Bernie?" I spoke as I entered the door.

"Hi Cade, no you're on time. I'm waiting for Bernie and Miles to return from the bathroom. He took the little fella just before we got the all clear to go to the observation point. They should be back shortly. Do you want to see how we spent our morning? I have it on videotape."

"Sure." He pulled out the miniature videocam and started the tape. I looked at the viewing screen and saw Miles extending his hands, emitting a stream of fire from them that set off small explosions on the scattered objects along their path as they walked around the desert. I blinked and opened my mouth in shock.

"This is fun," he squealed in delight as one heated boom after another was set off, consuming stacks of cardboard and wooden boxes in addition to mounds of debris in a blaze of fire. Childlike sandcastles and volcanoes erected with small firecracker sticks placed in the center of them were ignited and exploded, flinging particles of sand on the lens of the camera. Without thinking that I was in no danger of being hit by a plume of sand and dust, I flinched and jerked away from the screen.

"What the hell Todd?"

"I thought the same thing Cade, but who am I to tell a man how to raise his son? Miles said you knew he could create fire and you had seen him do it. He said it was a part of his self- defense training and he showed us some moves his companion Angelique had taught him. I had to admit he was good at it. I was concerned about the possibility of an accident happening, but Bernie told me you and Lecia were raising Miles as some free-spirited, free-range kid. I know you're not an average kind of guy, so I thought you didn't want to raise an average kid. Trust me, Miles is no average kid." I ran my hands through my hair.

*When I get my hands on that kid of mine, he's not going to be average.* I looked around the room and turned my head to the door, hoping the noise on the other side was them returning from the bathroom, but no one opened the door.

"Shouldn't they be back by now? It shouldn't take this long." I paced the room.

"Where could they be?" I placed my hands in my pockets and Todd shrugged.

Finally the door opened, and I looked up at Bernie, who entered in a rush and began scanning his eyes around the room.

"Did Miles come back here? I looked outside around the bathroom and couldn't find him. Hi Cade."

"No, we thought he was still with you. What took you so long Bernie?"

"Well, I had a little more business to attend to than I had originally planned, and Miles said he would wait outside the door for me after it got a little warm in the bathroom."

"Maybe he wandered around and went to the observation point. Let's go and look for him there," Todd suggested as we gathered our things and exited the door in time to hear directions over the loudspeaker.

"Attention on set. Attention on set. Actors to your positions and all other personnel to the observation booth. Fifteen minutes till shooting."

"See, I told you he probably went to the observation point. Come on, let's hurry up over there." We all began sweating in the hot sun beaming on us, but I was also anxious as it crossed my mind that he may not be there, when we arrived.

The triple-sized trailer was cool, filled with windows for observing the action, and perched inside a carved-out large trench with sandbags piled up in front of it for protection. My heart fell to the pit of my stomach and I grabbed myself to stop from hurling my breakfast, as I was consumed immediately with nerves, after a quick survey of the room revealed no trace of Miles.

"Miles! Miles!" I called his name throughout the room, drawing the attention of a man sitting in the director's chair.

"Quiet man. You're a guest of the production company and I could have you thrown off set, but it's too late to safely do it."

"T-minus ten minutes," an assistant called out on the set; and I ran to the director to attempt to halt the filming until we could locate Miles.

"Sir, could you delay the shooting? We can't find my son." I grabbed his arm and he pulled away.

"Let go of me. Listen, I know you're Cade Moore of Fortune, but I'm working here, and this filming could cost a lot of money if we delay it. The set has already been cleared for safety and our stunt guy Brent is in the car."

I looked out the window and scanned around to see if I could see Miles, and no one was moving outside the window. I viewed a fancy blue sports car parked a small city block away.

"We have the set rigged with multiple liters of fuel, twenty-six detonators, and a few kilograms of black and flash powder for maximum effect." One of the tech guys came over and spoke to us, smiling and rubbing his hands.

"Look, the car is moving already." The eager tech guy pointed out the window.

I looked out the window and the car had started to move at a snail's pace, down the vacated street and toward the large building that was going to be destroyed.

"This will be a cinematic marvel. The explosion won't be the largest in recorded history, but we have it programmed to detonate in a series of nonstop fireballs. The car has been mounted on safety rails so that it won't flip so quickly from the blast of the explosions. The computer simulations we have planned will make the car appear closer to the building than it really is."

The trailer door opened, and everyone turned their attention to the man whose appearance caused their jaws to drop.

"Brent? If you're here, who's that in the car?"

"I want to know who in the hell locked me in my trailer. I had to break the door to get out." Brent placed his hands on his hips and looked around the room. The director turned his attention back to the action. "Get me a close up!" he screamed at the cameramen.

*No, no. Please no.* I closed my eyes, and despite my pleadings, I looked at the monitor in front of the director's stand and saw the face of my son; with an oversized helmet on his head as he looked into the camera, and his body was clothed in an oversized race car driver's jacket.

"What the shit is going on? Who is that kid and how did he get on my set?"

"He can't drive! Get someone to stop the car, now!" I looked around at Bernie and Todd, about to exit the trailer, just as the car sped up to about fifty miles an hour.

"Stay in here. The car is a self-drive model with a remote start up and it can't be stopped at this point. He doesn't need to know how to drive a car since it has been programmed to accelerate, the minute he touches the pedal," the director explained.

"He was pretending to drive my car earlier and he knew if he moved the seat closer to the steering wheel, he could tap the pedal." Bernie answered the question running through my head.

"I've got to get out of here and get to my son."

"I told you dammit to stay in here until after the explosion. It's not safe out there now."

"Explosion in four, three, two—" one of the grips yelled across the room, followed by a loud series of booms, and several of the flimsily constructed buildings blew up in paroxysmal flames while red, yellow, and orange fireballs flew into the air as the car sped away from the burning building. The adjacent buildings were hit with high-speed air cannons that blew them away in a blast of tumbling life-sized walls falling like dominoes, which worsened the visual illusion of mayhem.

"Wow!" High fives and hoots of excitement spread throughout the room as the car came to a stop away from the blast. I shook in fear and my heart was hurting as it thumped in my chest. My face dripped in sweat and my clothes were wet to my underwear as I waited for the all clear. The director calmed down in the midst of the backslaps and he looked at the car, still upright and on the metal tracks as it came to a complete stop.

"Boss, remember you told me to put kerosene in the trunk, to blow up the car in a surprise counterattack, as a plot twist?"

"Yeah, so?" The director's mouth slowly dropped open as his eyes rolled back and he slapped the side of his head.

"You've got to get the kid out of there before it blows!" One of the visual effects' guys screamed at him.

"We timed it, to give Brent five minutes to get out of the car, before it blows." A second grip confirmed my worst nightmare. I headed for the door and started running toward Miles as fast as I could, frantically waving my hands the whole time and hoping I got his attention.

"Miles, get out of the car! Get out of the car!" I tried yelling but began coughing and choking on the cloud of dust that hadn't settled and was falling on my face and clothes.

"Miles! Miles!" The car door finally opened, and Miles got out of the car and began jumping up and down.

"Ah, hah, hah, hah!" I heard him laughing as I got closer and began motioning for him to come to me, but he just kept jumping up and down, hitting the side of the car and throwing his fists triumphantly into the air. I made it to the car; and only the adrenaline coursing through my body stopped me from passing out from all the heat and my exhaustion.

"Ah, hah, hah, hah!" He continued laughing out loud as I ran to him full speed and grabbed him around his waist, while running away from the car. I dove with him in my arms and rolled down a sand embankment, into a bunker with him on top of me, just as the car exploded in a loud boom and burst into flames.

I closed my eyes and my throat burned as I gasped for air and tried to catch my breath. Miles's smiles faded as he cast his attention on the debris falling to the ground around us and he began struggling for air.

"Pops, Pops. Are you alright?" He placed his hand on my arm and hovered over me.

"I'll. Be. Alright." I sat up with his help. "You're okay?"

"I'm good Pops. This is the best day of my life." He threw his fists in the air. "Let's move to California. This place is the bomb."

"The bomb? Interesting choice of words son."

"Cade, you didn't say much at dinner and you seem so distant, like you're lost in your own thoughts. You also haven't asked how my day went or shared what happened with the negotiations."

I took another sip of my stiff drink and exhaled a deep breath before I looked at Lecia and intentionally looked away from Miles. The more I thought about the events of the day, the angrier I got, and I didn't want to risk saying something that would irreparably fracture my relationship with my son or my wife, but I had to tell Lecia. But I didn't know how.

In the limo on the way back, Miles had said, "Please don't tell Mami. It can be our secret Pops. I've kept your secrets." Indeed he had kept secrets, but for the past year, they'd been simple, like both of us going out for ice cream before dinner.

"Miles, you may be young, but you're not naïve. You can't believe that we share the same kind of secrets. Eating ice cream before dinner won't get you killed and what you did today could have cost you and others their lives."

"I'm sorry Pops and it won't happen again but please don't tell on me."

Our back and forth had continued all the way back to LA.

"Stop it Miles, and don't say another word about it." I sat back in my seat and looked out the window silently lost in my thoughts.

*How are we going to handle this?* I took a deep breath and hoped something would come to mind soon.

# CHAPTER SEVENTEEN

"We've been on this plane for almost an hour and the two of you have barely said anything to each other. I know it's been a long day for all of us but Cade, you're the one who insisted we return to North Carolina as soon as possible. Why was it so important to you to track down Miles's doctor who is at a conference in Charlotte? What is going on? One of you needs to talk to me—and right now."

I opened my mouth to speak while Miles sat quietly in the corner writing in his composition journal. I wouldn't have been surprised if my name was written at the top of his list. Lecia's phone began ringing, giving me some time to gather my thoughts. She looked at it on the table and immediately grabbed it.

"Wait a minute. This is Dana and she rarely calls me while we're on the road, unless it's something I need to know as soon as possible. Hi Dana. What's going on?"

"Hi Lecia. Please take me off speakerphone while we talk."

"Sure." She pressed the speaker button and Dana's voice disappeared from the room. Her request got my attention and I sat up, waiting for Lecia to share with me what had happened.

Lecia got up and went to the bedroom and I followed her and closed the door.

"Place the call on speaker. I want to hear this." She pressed the speaker button again and placed the phone on the bed.

"Dana, I'm on the jet in the bedroom and Cade is here with me."

"Where's Miles?"

"He's in the forward cabin and he can't hear you."

"Alright, I just heard from one of the mothers in my exercise class, who is the cousin of Miles's friend William in Maryland, that he died five days ago in an accidental fire. I understand he sustained third-degree burns and his funeral was three days ago. The school is planning a memorial service for him tomorrow, and I wanted to call you to let you know and give you time to decide how you wanted to break the news to Miles. I confirmed the news before I called, and I can send a picture of the poor child's obituary."

"Hi Dana. Thanks for calling us with the news, and I'm saddened to hear it. William Major was one of the first friends Miles made at the Institute's school and he shared a form of Miles's condition.

"Everything else is okay Dana?"

"Yes Cade, we're all fine, and before I forget to tell you Lecia, your parents can make it to Miles's gathering for potential investors."

"What are you talking about Dana?" She dried her eyes and looked at the phone.

"Miles called his Papi and his Granddaddy, and they agreed to listen to his proposal to invest in his new band in California. All members of the immediate family will be there. I think he planned to perform a song."

"Dana, let me get back to you. We haven't had a chance to talk about relocating to California and at the very least, let Miles be a part of a band." I placed my arm around Lecia's shoulder as she leaned against my chest, sad and tearful. She knew Miles's friends better than I did and it would probably be me who broke the news to him.

"I'm sorry I had to call with such sad news, but I thought Miles needed the chance to go to the memorial service if you got back in time. I'll let you all talk. Goodbye."

"Bye Dana." I ended the call and Lecia cried a few moments before drying her eyes.

"We need to prepare our son before this plane lands. I'll talk to him Cade, while you talk to the captain about altering our flight plans, if you want to keep the appointment with his doctor in Charlotte."

"Yes, I think we should keep the appointment but first go to Maryland after we find out the time of the memorial service, then fly out to Charlotte. Miles is the last appointment of the day. His doctor is a speaker at a conference in Charlotte but he's also providing consultation at the Levine Children's Hospital. He agreed to see Miles there. Are you sure you don't want to tell him together Lecia?"

"No, I can handle it Cade, but we need to confirm our new plans as soon as possible." Her phone pinged again, and it was an attachment from Dana with a copy of William Major's obituary with his smiling face on the cover of it.

"Let me go talk to the pilots. I'll be right back." I got up and left her in the bedroom. I hoped she remained in there until I returned. I passed through the main cabin and Miles looked at me.

"Did you tell Mami what I did?"

"No Miles, not yet." I kept walking to the cockpit to share the change in plans with the captain and the flight crew.

Miles was in Lecia's arms sobbing while she attempted to comfort him by the time I returned to the main cabin.

"I told him about William. I wasn't sure how long it would take for you to discuss the plans with the captain and I felt he needed to know as soon as possible."

"Mami, it's not fair. Why was William taken away from us when mean, hateful people are still here living their lives? William was a good person and he taught me sign language, so we could talk to his little brother who's deaf."

"I know it doesn't seem fair Miles, but that's not the nature of life. It's a good thing to be kind to others, but it doesn't guarantee any of us a long life. Remember, I lost my brother when we were only three years old. I know it hurts to lose those we love, but we have to draw together as a family to help each other through the hard times."

My heart ached as I watched the two of them embrace, trying to ease the pain of their suffering in the face of the senseless loss. I took him from Lecia's arms and found every nerve in my body quivering as I recalled the events of this afternoon. The realization that we could have been the parents mourning the loss of a child overwhelmed me. I buried my face in his hair and held him tight as we both needed the skin-to-skin contact as confirmation that even though I'd been angry with him earlier, I was there for him and would never stop loving him. Lecia gave us both sweet kisses but looked at me quizzically, since my response did seem out of proportion to my relationship with William when he was alive. I had heard Miles speak of his friend, but it was Lecia who had the most contact with the brothers and their family. Miles fell asleep and I knew I had to answer her questions; why I had refused to communicate earlier and why I had become overwhelmed with emotions at the loss of a child I really didn't know.

"Let me walk with Miles and help him in bed and then I'll be back. I have something I have to show you."

"Come son, let's go to bed. It's been a long day and we have a lot to do tomorrow." I helped him to his feet and escorted him to the bedroom where I held him again and gave him a kiss.

"I'll be right outside the door with Mami. Get some rest son." He got under the covers without protesting and closed his eyes. I hovered over him for a few minutes and heard him lightly snoring by the time I made it to the door, which I made sure I closed behind me. I guess the excitement of the day had tired him.

"Cade, what is going on between you and Miles? Both of you have been acting oddly since you came back from the desert. Did anything happen while the two of you were on the set?"

"I've been pondering how to tell you, and I guess the best way is to show you. I have a tape of Miles's first and only take on the movie set today."

"What? You were able to get him a role as an extra today? I'm sure he was excited." She smiled at me and looked on eagerly as I pulled out Todd's handheld video camera and let the tape roll. There was the closeup of Miles in the car speeding down the street and she turned to look at me, jaw dropped in shock, and then looked back at the video.

"What the hell is going on Cade? Is this a special effect? Tell me Miles wasn't really in that car speeding down the street."

"It wasn't a stunt." Before I could explain further, the first explosion occurred, causing her to grab her hair and pull at the roots while she screamed.

"Oh my gosh. Who thought this was a good idea to endanger the life of a child—my child, any child?"

"Lecia—" then the second explosion occurred, and I lowered my head in shame. I couldn't look at her because I still wasn't able to explain it to my own satisfaction. I saw her, out of the corner of my eye, open her mouth to speak then place her fist to her lips.

"I can't watch any more of this and I can't give you the benefit of the doubt that there is a good reason for this because there is none."

We both looked up as the door opened and Miles stood before us rubbing his eyes.

"I keep waking up. I don't want to stay in the room by myself."

Lecia got up and went to him but looked back to speak to me.

"Let's all go to bed together. Maybe things will seem clearer in the morning."

I doubted it, but I wasn't turning down an invitation to be in the same bed with my family. I knew I wasn't in the doghouse yet, but I would be yelping for mercy under the doghouse soon. I hoped Lecia was right. Maybe things would seem clearer in the morning. Right now, we still had each other and that was the thing I needed to focus on.

"I agree it's better if we go to bed." I hurried to join them as the plane raced back to Maryland to attend the memorial service tomorrow.

# CHAPTER EIGHTEEN

The day was long and the action nonstop, but I was determined to teach Miles by example, the importance of following through on commitments. I pulled the car into my parents' driveway and came to a stop before cutting the engine. Stifling a yawn, I pretended to clear my throat instead and gathered my things.

"Cade, don't you think we've done enough for one day? We flew in from the west coast in the wee hours of the morning, attended a memorial service for a child, which still has me emotionally drained, took Miles to his doctor for an examination which you, by the way, insisted on, and now you want Miles to perform for the family?" She counted off each event with her fingers and raised one eyebrow, daring me to say yes while I refused to make eye contact with her. Instead, I looked ahead at the landscape around the home I had seen hundreds of times before but never took the time to notice. The flowing fountain and shrubs we'd planted around it as kids to celebrate Father's Day so many years ago, provided the calm I needed for this day. I took a breath and unbuckled my seat belt.

"Lecia, I'm aware of how tiring this day has been. I've been with you the entire time. I get it, but since Miles called the family together without our knowledge or consent to perform for them, he needs to keep his word and perform. If he wants to form a band and possibly be a professional someday, he needs to understand one of the important rules of the business: the show must go on."

"I'm not tired Mami," Miles added and yawned. "But it's not just a performance Pops, it's a prospective investors' meeting."

"Where did you get that idea Mijo?" Lecia turned and looked back at him.

"You remember Parker—Parker Middleton—one of the kids I met on the cruise?"

Lecia nodded her head.

"Well, he said if he was going to be my manager, I had to have the funds for a band because I needed equipment. Pops was angry about the movie and not talking to me and I was also afraid Mami that you would say no after Pops told you about what happened; so I called Granddad and Papi and they said they would at least listen to me explain why I needed the money. Parker said I should show Papi and Granddad what they were paying for, so I decided I would sing and dance." He opened the car door and exited the vehicle with us, to continue the conversation on the paved driveway, leading to the front of the home.

"I'm still trying to process what little I saw of the video, and I was more frightened than angry Miles. You also need to understand that I never want you to intentionally place yourself or others in harm's way."

"I understand Mami, and I didn't want to get hurt, but the man said it would be fun. He promised me, and he was right; it was fun." My chest began to heave and my skin warmed, as I looked down at my son, telling me how placing his life in danger was fun.

"Enough about that Miles. You keep talking about this man that no one knows about. This man came up to you, took you to the car, and gave you the outfit, including a helmet?"

He didn't flinch under my interrogation, not this time or the first time I asked him on the way to the memorial service earlier today.

"Yes, Pops, that's what happened. You know I don't lie." He placed his small roller bag on the ground and took it by the handle and began rolling it up the driveway.

"Come back here young man. I'm not finished speaking to you." He turned around and came back to me. *You may not lie but you're not above manipulating a situation.*

"Cade let's not do this again. You know Miles has never lied to us and he's insulted that we keep asking him the same thing. He has your stubborn pride, and besides, your security detail did say that the stunt guy was locked in his dressing room and the door was barricaded. Let's just go inside, let Miles perform, then we can call it a day." Lecia looked between the both of us and pursed her lips effectively, calling a halt to the testosterone standoff between me and our son.

"You're right Lecia, and Miles, I'm not calling you a liar. I'm just trying to figure out what happened; so that something like that never happens again. There was a security breach somewhere because very few people knew we had a VIP pass, and I plan to find out where it happened, but that's not your problem." I placed my hand on his shoulder and looked him in the eye, and he placed his hand on top of mine; our special signal to each other that we were okay with each other for now. The door opened, and my parents stood at the entryway, waving for us to come inside.

I found Vincent alone and busy at work in the family's entertainment room.

"Hi Vincent." I went over to join him on the makeshift stage.

"Hi Cade. Thanks for giving me the heads up about what happened in California, and I agree that the incident on the movie set was something sinister and aimed at killing Miles. The Network is on it, investigating everybody, including the folks assigned to protect your family."

"Thanks Vincent. I won't rest until I know that Miles and Lecia are safe." He nodded as I looked around the room where Miles was going to perform for the family.

"You didn't have to go to all the trouble of setting this up for Miles. It's just a small gathering for family where he gets a chance to sing and dance." I followed him as he walked around the room, testing mics for sound and adjusting the heights before we returned to the sound mixing board he had set up at the back of the room.

"I had your back when you decided to pursue a career in music, and my nephew needs to know I have his. There are no small performances, just as they're no small expressions of spirit. When that son of yours sings and dances, he shares his gift with others, which in turn enlarges the expression of spirit in everyone around him. I don't know how else to describe it, but it's a spiritual experience watching him. I'm telling you Cade; the boy is going to be on a big stage somewhere at some point in his life." I sighed and began helping him set up the musical instruments near the mics. I knew when my brother made up his mind to do something, there was no changing it.

"How was the memorial service for Miles's friend?" He didn't look up from the mixing board and continued his task as Miles's sound engineer.

"The kids and teachers were sad, as expected, but William's mother said something interesting to me and Lecia while we were extending our condolences to her. You know William had a condition like Miles's; he could withstand high heat temperatures, but he couldn't create fire or withstand smoke inhalation. Anyway, she said William would still be alive if she had the money we had." My father came into the room while I was speaking to Vincent.

"She said we had money that she didn't have to keep Miles busy, so he wouldn't become obsessed and hurt himself playing with fire." Vincent looked up from the board for the first time, fully engaged in what I was saying to him.

"I remained silent and listened as she spoke, knowing that she was grieving, and I needed to respect the way she chose to grieve, but I wasn't going to feel guilty about sharing my resources with my kid." My father cleared his throat before interjecting his thoughts into the conversation.

"So now you understand why I wanted to share my resources with the two of you and why it angered me when you both refused my help. Now my grandson is seeking my help and I hope you understand, Cade, if I choose to give it to him."

"Dad, Lecia and I have some decisions to make that will affect Miles, and at this point, if he's interested in things that aren't dangerous and it keeps him occupied, we probably will support it."

"What's going on Cade?" my father asked as Vincent turned his attention back to the board. He was more familiar with Miles's condition than my father was.

"We'll talk about it later Dad." I chose not to answer after I saw Dana and the kids coming into the room and heading to me for hellos and hugs.

"Hi kids. Come here and give your uncle some love." They all took their turn welcoming me home.

"The food is almost ready and Lecia's parents have arrived. They're in the kitchen putting the food they brought out on the tables."

"Why?" I hunched my shoulders and held my open palms in the air.

"Miles wanted a meet-and-greet after the performance to network with his investors, so he called both of his grandmothers, who would never turn down the opportunity to prepare food for the children, and Grammie heard about it and began baking so many pies that her house began to look like a bake-off, and—"

"Wait Dana, there's more?" She nodded.

"Lauren's twin brothers and their families are coming over later tonight. They all had plans and couldn't make the performance but agreed to come by later tonight."

"Don't you think you all are indulging Miles, a little too much?"

"And the problem would be?" my father asked and Lecia's voice ran across my mind as she had voiced her concerns many times about my family overindulging our son.

"Where is Tia Lecia and Miles?" Aria asked just as he entered the room with Lecia, her parents, and the rest of the family. Miles took his place behind the lead mic, and my oldest nephew, Alex, took a mic from his father and turned it on.

"If you all will take a seat, we can start the show." Miles positioned his mic, and Vincent got up for last-minute adjustments of Aria's mic, who was providing lead background vocals while her sister Lexi danced and sang in the background. Alex was on the bass and Austin went to take a seat at the drums. The adults took their seats in chairs around the family's large entertainment room in the basement, and Alex spoke again into the mic and strutted around like a ringleader at a PT Barnum event.

"Ladies and gentlemen, this is the *wooorld* premiere. I present to you, Miles Moore and his revue." We started clapping and the spotlight went on Miles, who began performing favorite family tunes the kids had practiced many times before. The door opened, and Doris entered, surprising the adults, but it appeared the kids were in on it when Alex gave his mic to her and she joined them on the stage to provide additional background vocals. At that moment, it felt like I was being transported back to earlier times in my own life, when we were kids and spent too many nights to count, entertaining our parents. I looked over at my father and Lecia's father, both were beaming with pride as the kids performed. Miles had his investors right where he wanted them. My kid may not have exercised the best judgment in riding in a car speeding down a set filled with explosives, but he wasn't dumb. He knew how to play to his investors.

I turned my attention back to the performance when the volume in his voice started to fade. He was making a rookie mistake, in dancing and singing away from the microphone but still doing a good job. Lecia and I didn't want to necessarily encourage this new venture, but we didn't want to discourage it either. I looked at her and watched her clapping to the beat of the music as I rose from my seat and placed the additional guitar over my shoulder and I began playing. I motioned to the background singers to raise the volume of their voices to fill in the gap while Miles caught his breath and made his way back to the mic. Just as he had seen me do many times before in my performances, I made a motion with my head and pointed to members of the band.

"Ladies and gentlemen, Alex Moore on the bass," he pointed to his cousin and he started his solo, followed by applause from the adults.

"Give some love to Austin Moore on drums," Miles spoke into the mic and Austin broke out into a lively percussion solo. I had been working with Austin since he was three years old and he was very good on drums and bongos.

"My beautiful ladies of song, let's hear it for them." Miles continued and Doris, a gifted singer, took the lead, then let our nieces display their vocal talent before they all joined in, to end the performance. The family was all on their feet clapping and singing with tears of joy. It was a spiritual experience, as we all lifted our voices, grateful for the communion with each other. I loved when we all got together, but the offer to relocate to California was an excellent opportunity for all of us, even if it meant separating from our extended family members. The music ended; and I thought this was the end until Miles spoke into his mic again.

*My boy has a lot of talent.*

I hated to admit it, but my mind was locked in a battle of wanting to grab him in an affectionate bear hug of support or to warn him about the challenges of child performers who have ended up, in a self-destructive heap at the altar of the fame monster. My attention wandered as I played well-known guitar chords, but I returned to the present moment at the sound of his voice.

"Wait, it's not over. I have a surprise. Start the recording Uncle Vincent." He spoke over the applause that calmed, as the lights dimmed, and the video of the movie scene shot yesterday came on, with Miles racing down the street in a sports car just before the buildings exploded on the big screen. Animation was suspended as the adults who were standing stiffened their posture as if they were frozen in place, followed by drop-jawed expressions of disbelief at what they were seeing. The kids' attention gazed upon the screen with wide eyes and nervous giggles while Miles jumped up and down with glee. *He still doesn't get it.*

"Ah, hah, hah, hah!" That laugh again filled the room. I hated that laughter—the sound of his clueless folly. The video ended, and the lights came up so that Miles could see, for the first time, I'm guessing, the feelings of the adults in his life in addition to me and Lecia who loved him and would always be there to support him. All his grandmothers took a seat, placed a hand over their hearts, and silently shook their heads. Dana went over to Lecia and gave her a hug.

"Lecia, I'm so sorry and my heart goes out to you. I'm assuming you've seen this before."

"I have, and it doesn't get any easier seeing it again." I looked at Miles as he searched the room and looked at the faces of the adults. His face of glee slowly turned to sad puppy-dog eyes and he sunk his shoulders low and hung his head.

"Listen, I'm getting too old for this and my heart can't take this kind of excitement. Miles, say what you need to say to your investors and you and I need to go to add a new word to that notebook you like carrying around. We'll be talking about self-control." The kids looked at Miles and the initial expressions of awe and respect for his boldness slowly disappeared.

"I have pies available to sweeten the directness of what I plan to say to all of you children."

"But Grammie," the children let out a chorus of moans. I sat back and took Lecia's hand as my grandmother spoke out of turn—as she was known to do at family gatherings. I wasn't sure how we were going to handle this issue with

Miles, but I was grateful my grandmother was pointing us in the right direction. My father spoke up next.

"Miles, your performance was fantastic, but I can't say I've ever thrown money away in a reckless venture, and your behavior was reckless. What possessed you to get in that car?" The other adults looked at him as he continued to lower his head. "I can see by the look on your parents' faces that they didn't give you permission to do what you did."

"The man on the movie set said it would be fun, Granddad." Miles answered.

"I agree with Charles Aiden on that. You're my only grandchild, and I was proud that you came to me for help. You know we're here for you, but we need some assurances before we give you funding." Lecia's father spoke next. "Is that some sort of crazy thing kids are doing now?"

"I promise I won't do anything like that again. I love music way more than being in the movies. I need money for instruments and for a band," Miles began pleading with them.

"We had VIP tickets and that's how we got on the set, but he shouldn't have been allowed to get into the car and I'm having the whole thing investigated." I tried to deflect some of the attention away from Miles. His eyes were filling with tears and I thought he finally understood why we were concerned about the incident.

"So you'll keep your grades up and no more shenanigans?" my father asked, and Miles nodded. "Well then, we can talk later about funding."

"I will support you also, but why did you ask for so much money? You already have equipment and instruments," Lecia's father added.

"These people can't work for free, and anyone I hire in California won't work for free," Miles answered and waved his hands at his family band behind him.

"California?" Another chorus of comments filled the room and I quickly got up to move him and the action along.

"Miles, go with Grammie and maybe if you eat a good dinner, she'll hold off on the self-control lecture at least for tonight. I want to thank all of you for your honest reactions to the video. I think Miles now realizes the consequences of his actions and, for the first time, I hope he sees the affect his behavior has on others."

"I get it Pops. I didn't mean to frighten you and Mami. It's just that the man on the set said it was going to be fun." He repeated his statement about the man.

"Go with Grammie. We can talk about all of that later."

"I think I'll go get something to eat too. I'm hungry." Doris started toward the door—leave it to her to disappear just when things get a little uncomfortable.

I got up and began ushering Miles and the other children out of the room with Grammie. I made sure they were out of earshot before resuming control of the conversation.

"Lecia and I were scared shitless." My mother wrinkled her brow and shot me the Lauren-isn't-pleased-with-your-language look. "I meant we were frightened out of our wits, and not sure what to do but I think you all have impressed upon Miles, what we couldn't seem to get him to understand and for that, we're grateful."

"We're glad we could help, but what about the California thing?" My father was not swayed by my attempts to control the narrative. Lecia blew out a breath and rubbed the side of her face just as Miles came back in the room.

"Mami, I don't mean to be a handful, honestly," he came to her with remnants of sweet potato pie stuck to the sides of his lips.

"Why do you think you're a handful?" she asked as he looked at her, his eyes glistening and sadness appearing.

"Senora Lydia said you can't have more children because I'm such a handful." Lecia's eyes rolled and her head fell back before she blew out a breath and pulled Miles into the chair with her.

"You aren't the reason why I haven't had more children, and we've had the discussion before about other adults talking to you about adult matters. What did we say, you were supposed to do if that happened?"

"Tell you about it." She cupped his face and looked into his eyes before giving him a kiss on the cheeks.

"I would be one happy woman if I had one hundred children like you Miles."

"Well, I don't want one hundred brothers and sisters, but maybe one will do." We all laughed with him.

"Leave it to Lydia to cause trouble even if it's from the grave," Marisela shook her head while she spoke and Lecia's father and I agreed.

"Are you all coming to my meet-and-greet? We have plenty of good food."

"Sounds like a good idea son." I grabbed him by the hand and headed for the door. "Come on guys, our little star wants his audience to come celebrate with him."

He was a handful, but his timing was perfect. Lecia seemed to be leaning towards the thought of relocating to California if I was reading her correctly. Miles's doctor told us at his appointment earlier today that he was probably going to relocate his practice to North Carolina, but I knew Lecia didn't want to get enmeshed in family affairs if we moved back to North Carolina, and I wasn't ready to discuss with everyone that there was a high likelihood that this time next year, we would probably be living in California.

Michele Sims

# CHAPTER NINETEEN

"Thanks Dr. Hansen, for helping us with the transition to a new treatment team in California. I guess this will be our last meeting with you before we leave." We were meeting with the treatment team including Miles's favorite therapist, Dr. Brian at the children's hospital in Charlotte.

"You all will be in good hands with the team there, but I have to admit, I'll miss seeing you Miles." He squirmed in the chair and smiled at his doctor.

"We've gone over the results of the tests and the laboratory explorations of Miles's current fire load production and the projections for his fire load production as an adult. Currently, Miles has the fire load that can start a fire and completely burn down objects the size of your average car, and as an adult, we project he'll have the fire load to destroy most small buildings at the low end of his fire load production." Miles began smiling broadly and bounced in his seat.

"Ah, hah, hah, hah!" *There's that dastardly sound of menacing laughter again.* Lecia placed a hand on his leg above his knee to settle him down.

"Dr. Hansen, I'm starting to wonder if it was a good idea to include him in the discussion from the looks of his response to the news."

"Mr. and Mrs. Moore, that's exactly why I recommended to include him in this discussion. Miles needs to understand the extent of his abilities and learn methods of self-control."

"There's that word again, self-control." Miles sat back in his seat.

"Miles, do you think that's a bad word?" Dr. Brian leaned over and looked at him.

"No, it's just that I got a lot of homework from Grammie Mommy and I had to discuss it with her."

"Grammie Mommy?" Dr. Hansen asked.

"That's my grandmother, his great-grandmother. Miles, please don't interrupt. Let Dr. Hansen ask you questions and then we can all ask our questions."

"Alright," He grabbed his notebook, a pencil and prepared to answer questions from members of his team. Dr. Hansen went first.

"Miles, did you look up the word cauldron like we asked you to?" He opened his notebook and began reciting the answer.

"Cauldron- a large metal pot with a lid and handle used for cooking especially on an open fire."

"Very good Miles. You're very bright and this will be easy for you to understand."

"Doctor, a cauldron could also be a situation characterized by instability and strong emotions, like a cauldron of hot anger," Lecia added.

"That's also correct Mrs. Moore, and the two meanings illustrate what we've been trying to explain to Miles. We want him to help contain his powers and develop a protective cauldron to control it, instead of letting his emotions control him. Children with Miles's condition need to understand it and the consequences of having powers like he has. The team in California have developed an excellent program to teach them fire safety, and there are plenty of desert locations to let them discharge some of the fire energy. We have had former patients who've been coerced to use their powers for destruction and criminal activities. We don't want the same thing to happen to Miles."

"Doctors, how involved are the parents in the program?" Lecia addressed her concerns to the team.

"Parents are encouraged to be very involved and as I shared with you earlier, there is a part-time opening for a nurse practitioner if you're interested in applying and finding out first hand."

"Thanks for letting me know about the opening, and I did get an offer after I applied."

"There are two teams in the program and you won't be assigned to Miles's team so that your role in his care will exclusively be as a parent and not a staff member. I want to give Dr. Brian a chance to finish discussing his concerns."

"Miles and I have been working on his anger issues so that he doesn't produce fire in response to irritation or a need for vengeance. His new team will continue to work with him on ways to harness his power and use it for good."

"Dr. Brian, I already know I can create music, write stories, and play with my soldiers and my other toys."

"Yes, Miles, your music is a gift, another special power that you can use for good and to spread love and happiness to others."

"I understand Dr. Brian."

"I hope we have helped you understand that while you have special powers, you have a human body that can be bruised and injured; and people can get hurt if they don't understand the condition."

"You mean like William?" Miles asked and placed his notebook in his lap.

"Yes, like William and countless others. Miles, I want you to live a life of balance, be a kid, and not feel you have to be some superhero trying to save the world." He laughed, the usual infectious laughter that causes others to join in even if it's a private joke.

He smiled before he responded.

"I understand what you're saying Dr. Brian, but a superhero gig sounds like fun."

*Only my nine-year-old son would use the word gig.* I understood that although he didn't always show it, he was listening to the things I said.

It was a chilly night and I started a fire, after we got back from the doctor's visit, and we sat around with our favorite drinks. Miles sipped on the contents of his apple juice box and stared at his notebook, while I sipped from a glass of wine.

"I've reviewed both offers, Lecia, and I think the California offer is the best one. What do the two of you think?"

"I've looked at both offers too and working part time with the medical team in California would be good for me now that Miles is older."

"I want to move to California too. I've already called Parker and Rashad to let them know I'm coming. Can we move tomorrow?"

"Not yet Miles. It takes some planning to move an entire household from the east coast to California, and we won't be there for another three to four weeks. But, in the meantime, we all promised to let go of something before we make the move. I'm going to burn the European contract and not look back. The band members are all excited about the move out west, now that we have built a solid fan base there." I tossed the contract for the European tour in the fire.

"I agreed to burn my day planner that I used to plan all the activities for me and Miles. I promise I'll give him more time to plan his own activities. You're a good boy Miles, and you've proven that you understand why, you can't do everything that impulsively comes to mind." She tossed the sheets of her day planner in the fire.

"I understand what self-control is now." He made no attempts to throw anything in the fire.

"You told me you planned to burn your list. You not only understand the concept of self-control, but we also talked about avoiding negative behaviors such as seeking vengeance." I thought he would tear out the pages with the names on his list, but he got up and tossed the entire notebook in the fire, and afterwards we all grabbed our drinks and watched the flames blaze.

"Will I get my own room downstairs, with a stone floor and a fireplace, in a room next to my bedroom like at Uncle Vincent's house?"

"Yes, your mother and I will look at the plans he has drawn up for us tomorrow." Lecia nodded her head in agreement.

"And I want a dog named Bailey." He swung his legs as he sat back in the chair, finishing his carton of juice.

"You have to prove you're ready for the responsibility of a dog Miles. I don't plan to clean up after you *and* a dog." Lecia placed her glass back on the table.

"You'll see Mami. I'll keep my room clean, keep my grades up, and get up to take care of my dog. I have a lot of energy and I can't wait to get to California." He came and sat on the couch in between us and laid his head on my chest. I knew we were going to be just fine as long as we had each other. What I didn't know, and the investigation thus far had provided little answers, was who wanted to hurt my son and who the man was who led Miles to the sports car. My security team had no clue, but we all agreed that the answer was to keep a close eye on Miles to make sure it didn't happen again.

# CHAPTER TWENTY

*Six weeks later.*

We landed at LAX on a commercial flight across country. We couldn't use the family's jet because my father needed it for his personal use and it belonged to him. Miles was not used to usual domestic travel and he was crankier than usual.

"Dad, when are we going to get our own jet?"

"I don't know Miles," I responded as we made our way off the gangway and down to baggage claim with the throng of humanity. There were cost overruns in moving an entire household and a band, and I wasn't about to shell out more money for a private jet.

"We have to get our bags too?" I turned and frowned at him.

"Miles, please stop asking so many questions and keep up or you'll need to hold my hand." Lecia intervened before we butted heads. She was good at responding to his whining, and after taking a bathroom break and getting him a snack, we had him take a seat and listen to his personal electronics while we got the bags.

I looked over while we waited and saw the cutest little girl dressed in a pink top, a matching tulle tutu skirt, and a tiara on her head. I chuckled and pointed her out to Lecia as she crossed her legs and rested her chin in the palm of her hand, so she could look at Miles with her big soft brown eyes. I couldn't hear their conversation, but she was animated like sunshine, rainbows, and unicorns all rolled up into one, while Miles respectfully gave her his attention and took the earbuds out of his ears.

"Allie." A man called out, and the little girl and a woman standing nearby, turned to the sound of the voice coming from a tall man, with an imposing image. At first, she smiled with her whole body, jumped up, and began walking with little lights shining on her tennis shoes before she broke out into a run with her thick ponytails bouncing in the air.

She squealed with delight and he picked her up into the air and twirled her around as she spread her arms like wings.

"You're making me fly Daddy." There was a twinkle in his eyes as he looked at her and planted kisses on her cheeks.

"I'll be right back Lecia. Don't try picking up the heavy bags. I've hired someone to come help us. I'll be over there checking on Miles."

"Alright but he looks fine."

I was drawn to the little girl with her daddy and went over to check on Miles, who had risen from his seat and was surrounded by the little girl and two adults who looked like her parents. I was surprised how patient Miles was with her, and his cranky mood that we were dealing with earlier had disappeared.

"Hello, I'm Cade, and this is my son Miles." I extended my hand to the man, who introduced himself as John and his wife Joan.

"And what's your name?" I smiled at the little girl, who moved closer to her father and planted herself against his leg.

"It's alright Princess. You can speak to strangers when I'm around."

It was at that point, I realized I might have been creating an awkward situation.

*Awkward, but they are talking to my son.*

"My name is Princess Allie. That's what my daddy calls me." She looked up at him and beamed a bright smile to him.

"You've been our princess from the day you were born baby girl." She patted him on the leg.

"Are we going to the fun park today Daddy?"

"Not today, but we'd better get going. I have a car waiting for us and I don't want it to get towed." He grabbed her by the hand and turned to me before they left.

"Miles told us you just relocated to California. I hope for the best for you and your family."

"Thank you, John." They began moving toward the exit after Allie started pulling on his hand.

We were on our way to our new home, taking the scenic route past iconic structures like the Hollywood sign high up in the hills, and I couldn't shake the image of John with his little princess. I guess I'd suppressed the desire for a larger family, including a little girl, now that nine years had passed since Lecia had given birth to Miles.

"What was that cute little girl at the airport telling you?" I looked at Miles through the rearview mirror as I negotiated LA's traffic and he looked back at me with the blankest look on his face. I wasn't sure which he didn't understand—cute or girl?

"Who are you talking about, Allie?'

"Yes Allie, that was her name." He rolled his eyes and huffed. *Cantankerous Miles is back.*

"She said a lot of things. Her father was a fire chief and he helped her win a poetry contest. They came to California to claim the grand prize, a trip to an amusement park."

"She was acting out something as she spoke to you."

"Yeah, that was part of her performance when she said her poem 'Dreams.' I guess you want me to tell you the poem?"

"I can't imagine you remembered it and no we don't expect you to tell us something you may have heard only one time." Lecia added.

"I remember it Mami." He cleared his throat and Lecia looked back at him and smiled.

"Starry nights, starry skies,
Turn in to dreams by day,
and magically,
we find a way,
to grow wings to fly high.
So dream big,
let those dreams take you,
to new moons.
Your dreams will come true,
maybe not today,
or even tomorrow,
but good things are,
heading your way,
soon and very soon."

We smiled as Miles finished presenting the gift, the little girl had left for all of us to enjoy.

"I'm hungry. Can we stop and get something to eat?" He smiled, and I knew he was going to love the surprise we had at the house waiting for him: a new puppy named Bailey. My manager had also run into the promoter for the Prince tour coming to LA next week and called to tell me he got three VIP passes to the concert.

*How is that for luck, or maybe it's just a coincidence.* Mother often told me what seemed to be coincidences in life were actually small gifts of the spirit, that should never be taken for granted or shrugged off.

*Luck or coincidence, either way, this is going to blow Miles's mind.*

I looked ahead at the massive traffic jam on the LA freeway and I knew, for better or worse, this would be my new reality. A new contract, an exciting tour schedule coming up soon, and a happy family, were the rewards for relocating to the City of Angels.

Michele Sims

# CHAPTER TWENTY-ONE

*One year later.*

The door opened and Lecia appeared, harried and dressed in a trench coat on a sunny, dry southern California day. Miles and I were engaged in a mortal battle in one of his video games and, of course, I wasn't winning. I put down the controller and looked up at Lecia, her hair pulled up in a messy bun and her face flushed as she untied the belt and got out of the coat. I had gotten a brief cryptic phone call from Pete minutes earlier, to expect she would be upset when she got home. He didn't share the details and hastily hung up the phone after a woman in the background kept pleading for his attention.

"Mami, why are you dressed like that?" Miles looked at her, curious as to why she was wearing a very short, French-styled maid costume. I was curious about it too and I sat back in my chair awaiting the answer. She didn't respond initially but seemed more interested in jerking open the closet door, forcibly placing the coat on the hanger and staring at the closed door before turning around to face us with fists at her side.

"Mami, why is your dress so short?" I leaned forward and saw the hint of black lace at the top of her thigh-high stockings, the curve of her thighs, and her buttocks hidden beneath a very short black skirt, topped with a tight white blouse.

"Mami was trying on her outfit for a masquerade party," I answered for her, which seemed to appease his curiosity. We had attended a masquerade party last week, so Miles was familiar with the concept. I got up and went to the bar to pour Lecia a glass of wine.

"Pops let's end the game now. You have no chance of winning and I need to go get my bag for my overnight with Parker."

"Make it a club soda Cade." I raised one eyebrow. Lecia loved a glass of wine, especially after a trying day, but she was declining it today, so I gave her a generous glass of cold soda and placed my hand on the small of her back to guide her to one of the chairs. I turned my head to hide the smile spreading across my face as I watched her vain attempts to position herself modestly in a chair with the outfit, which was much too short for sitting in plush chairs. She gave up trying to sit modestly and eventually settled on the edge of the chair and took a sip from her glass.

"Miles, I haven't given permission for you to go tonight. Remember, it depended on if you completed your chores." He turned toward her and began counting them off using his fingers.

"I fed and walked Bailey, who is asleep in the kitchen taking a nap, I cleaned my room, and I've finished my homework, and Pops gave me permission to go." Her head snapped in my direction.

"Lecia, remember you promised to give Miles a little more freedom to do things with his friends that didn't include Mommy, Miles, and friends? We've been here a year and you've not allowed him to go to a sleepover. He kept his part of the bargain and we weren't going to be home tonight anyway. You insisted on celebrating my birthday tonight downtown and letting Miles stay here with an attendant overnight."

"Miles, are you ready to go?" Kenneth Curtis, our chauffeur, came into the room. He was hired as the driver, but I liked his organizational skills and the way he helped Lecia set up our sprawling new home.

"Just a minute Mr. Curtis. Let me get my bag." He raced out of the room to get his things.

"I'll be heading home after I drop Miles off, so I'll say my goodbyes Mr. Moore and—Mrs. Moore." He looked at Lecia, not knowing what to make of her outfit, and quickly looked away.

"Good night Ken." I muffled a snicker as Lecia pulled on the hem of her skirt.

"Good bye Mami and Pops." Miles came back and we both hugged our smiling son, who raced out the door in front of Ken. In his short employment with us, Ken Curtis proved his loyalty by his hard work, and according to Miles, he was the bomb. I knew their bond was forged from Miles's secrets he felt Ken had kept, but, Ken had discretely funneled knowledge of his antics to us. I turned, faced Lecia, and inhaled the scent of perfume she wore when she wanted to tell me, she wanted me and needed sex, without using words.

"Cade, I thought we had plans to spend your birthday downtown at our favorite hotel. Why weren't you there?"

"Why didn't you answer my calls or return my messages, Lecia?" I went to the bar and fixed a drink. I took a sip and pulled out my phone to call her.

"I left messages and—" Her phone rang on the table near the kitchen.

"I left my phone Cade, when I had to run out to a doctor's appointment this morning. I forgot the appointment was today and I grabbed the wrong bag."

"You've been tired lately and looking pale. What did the doctor say?"

"I'll get to that Cade, but I still want to know why you ghosted on me? We've been slipping into a rut and I felt we needed to spice things up a bit."

"So that explains the outfit." She took another sip of her soda before placing the glass on the table in front of her. This time she sat back in the chair and my vision of her lovelies was unimpeded. I sat back opposite her and enjoyed the show she had gone to the trouble to arrange for my birthday.

"You've spiced things up just by wearing that outfit, so what happened?"

"Cade, I'm so embarrassed. At first, I blamed you for not being there, but I have no one to blame but myself."

"Lecia, you know I don't like a mystery so spill it."

"I went to the hotel room and knocked on the door expecting you to open it. I had taken off my coat and a pretty young woman opened the door. She yelled into the room, 'Honey, the girl is here.' I could hear water, like a shower was running, and I couldn't believe that you had changed the narrative of our sex game by adding a third person. She acted as if she was expecting me, and I was uncomfortable but decided to play along. The woman escorted me into the room and took off her robe and she was wearing a thong bikini outfit over her tight buns and perky breasts. I was prepared to give you a piece of my mind when the door opened and—"

"It was Pete." I blew out a breath and allowed her to finish telling me the story.

"Yes, and he came out, dressed in his boxers sporting a boner. I can't tell you how I felt in that moment, and the explanation only made it worse. It seems that he and this young lady were waiting for an exotic dancer to join the party and she thought I was her. How do we get past this Cade? I'm your wife dressed in a revealing costume, standing in front of a member of your band, who's standing in front of me with his cock peeking out of his underwear." I went to the chair, lifted her into my arms, and held her while she cried.

"Pete called and told me you stopped by the hotel. He was irritated with me because he thought I had told you he had the room and I told him I tried but I couldn't get in touch with you. He was embarrassed also, but I can assure you, he's been in tighter spots. He's willing to forget it if you will. I'm not as concerned about Pete right now as I am about you. How are you?"

"I'm tired and I want to get out of my masquerade outfit."

"Alright, let's go to the bedroom and relax a bit." I walked her down the hall and the lacy red underwear I loved seeing her in was lying on the bed where I had placed it. She stopped and looked at it.

"Don't worry about it. I wanted the visual delight of seeing you in it as my only birthday present."

"Did Pete describe the woman he was with? Young, beautiful and totally ego deflating, if I recall her image, and now I'm supposed to try to feel sexy, prancing around in this?"

"Alright, maybe not now, but you did ask me what I wanted for my birthday." I raised my brows and gave her my sexy smile. She looked at the bra and thong one more time before grabbing them and walking off to the bathroom while I stripped down to my boxers and settled back on the bed, awaiting her return. She came back wearing them and black stiletto heels with silver dangling earrings and a necklace to match, crowned with her sexy smile.

"You had a mood transformation in the bathroom? I'm liking it—no, correction—I'm loving it Lecia." She walked slowly toward me.

"I thought if I was going to do this, now was the time." I smiled as she placed a knee on the bed and swung her other leg over my pelvis. She looked as if I was in for a good ride, and boy was I ready.

"You wanted to do it for my birthday?" I grabbed her hips and smiled.

"That too, but I'm choosing to do it because in the next two months, I won't be able to wear this outfit."

"Why not babe?" She placed her hands on the side of my face and looked into my eyes.

"Because we're expecting again Cade. I'm pregnant." I sat up, stroked her hair, and ran my hands reverently along the sides of her face. Tears ran down my cheeks as I pressed my forehead to hers and tenderly kissed her lips.

"Lecia, we're pregnant?" She bit her lower lip and nodded.

"Yes, we're pregnant." Tears glistened in her eyes.

"How far along are you?" She sat back, her butt on my legs as we talked.

"About four weeks. I'm scheduled for an ultrasound on my next visit. I wanted you to be there with me for my first one."

"I wouldn't miss it. Why didn't you call me?"

"No phone, remember?"

"Right. Well, that might alter our plans to try something new tonight."

"Maybe, but I still want to dance for you. I've been feeling sexier today than I've felt in months. I don't care if my feet swell or that I won't have the slim shape of the women who come to see you perform. I just don't care about that anymore. We're having another baby and I didn't think this was going to happen for us again."

"You wouldn't have admitted it before tonight Lecia, but I know how sad it made you, no matter how much I told you it was alright for me, as long as I had you and Miles to come home to."

"You've been good about it Cade, and I know it was me who felt the sense of loss. Even as a little girl, I saw myself as a mother to many children, and now my dreams are coming true."

"The doctor said everything was alright?"

"Yes, but she told me to take it easy and relax. Dancing for me is relaxing, so turn on some music. I feel so free and fulfilled." She got up off the bed and began running her hands down the sides of her body. I turned on the music player I kept at my bedside and she began swaying to a slow, sultry jazz tune as I adjusted the pillows and placed my hands behind my head to enjoy the show.

The second song started, she was still dancing, graceful and rhythmic, in a trance like state of bliss, and I realized she was no longer dancing for me, but for herself. Lecia loved children and the idea that she was carrying another one, a child she had long hoped for and had brought us both unimaginable joy. I got off the bed hoping I'd break the trance.

"Lecia, honey, I don't want you to overexert yourself. It wouldn't be good for you or the baby if you dance her out of you."

"You said her. Wouldn't it be great if we had a little girl?"

"Yes, but I don't want to put pressure on myself if I didn't give you the right sperm."

"I'm glad you know it's on you, but a healthy second baby will be a blessing, boy or girl."

"Yes and you've given me the best birthday blessing, by arranging for me to impregnate you four weeks before my birthday, and I thank you—you're the greatest." We both laughed as I guided her back to the bed to rest, but she had something else in mind.

"That's just the start of what I have in mind for your birthday Cade. I love you with all my heart and soul, and time and time again, you've showed me how much you love me."

"I'll love you forever and into eternity." I kissed her, entwining my tongue with hers, and took her into my arms for a night of love—nice and slow was my specialty. As I held her against my chest, I looked into her sparkling brown eyes, beaming happiness at me like a laser and illuminating the dark corners of my soul. Lecia was my light—a bright ray of sunshine in my life—and I was lucky to bask in the glow of it. I kissed her tenderly, admiring the beauty of her spirit. Lecia was the woman I loved above all others, and I was grateful that she loved me too.

# ABOUT THE AUTHOR

Michele Sims is the creator of the Moore Family Saga and the Fire God Series. She loves writing hot love stories and women's fiction with multidimensional characters in multigenerational families. She is the recipient of the 2018 RSJ Aspiring Author Award and first runner up in the Introvert Press Poetry Contest for February 2018.  She is a member of the LRWA, in Charleston, SC and the From The Heart Romance Writers' online group.

She lives in South Carolina with her husband who has been her soulmate and greatest cheerleader. She is the proud mother of two adult sons and the auntie to many loved ones. When she's not writing, she's trying to remember the importance of exercise, travelling, listening to different genres of music, and observing the wonders of life on this marvelous planet.

Thank you for reading my book Playing with Fire. The prequel, Seed on Fire, and the third book in the Moore Family Saga, The Fire God Tour are also available.

If you enjoyed reading the book, please do me a favor and leave an honest review where you purchased it. Sign up at michelesims22.com with your email address for updates and giveaways.

Your support is appreciated.

www.ingramcontent.com/pod-product-compliance
Lightning Source LLC
Chambersburg PA
CBHW030737110726
47900CB00008B/2340